D0364771

RUN TO THE LEE

Publisher's Note

Works published as part of the Maryland Paperback
Bookshelf are, we like to think, books that have stood
the test of time. They are classics of a kind, so we
reprint them today as they appeared when first
published many years ago. While some social attitudes
have changed and knowledge of our surroundings has
increased, we believe that the value of these books as
literature, as history, and as timeless perspectives on
our region remains undiminished.

Also available in the series:
The Amiable Baltimoreans, by Francis F. Beirne
Mencken, by Carl Bode
The Lord's Oysters, by Gilbert Byron
The Potomac, by Frederick Gutheim
Spring in Washington, by Louis J. Halle
The Bay, by Gilbert C. Klingel
Tobacco Coast, by Arthur Pierce Middleton
Watermen, by Randall S. Peffer
Young Frederick Douglass, by Dickson J. Preston
Miss Susie Slagle's, by Augusta Tucker

RUN
TO THE
LEE

KENNETH F. BROOKS, JR.

THE JOHNS HOPKINS UNIVERSITY PRESS
BALTIMORE AND LONDON

© 1965 by Kenneth F. Brooks, Jr.
All rights reserved
Printed in the United States of America

Originally published, 1965, by W. W. Norton & Company
Johns Hopkins Paperbacks edition published 1988

The Johns Hopkins University Press
701 West 40th Street
Baltimore, Maryland 21211
˙The Johns Hopkins Press Ltd., London

LIBRARY OF CONGRESS CATALOGING-IN-PUBLICATION DATA

Brooks, Kenneth F.
Run to the lee.
(Maryland paperback bookshelf)
Reprint. Originally published: New York:
Norton, c1965.
1. Chesapeake Bay Region (Md. and Va.)—History.
2. Talbott, John, 1862–1929. 3. Albatross (Topsail schooner)
4. Schooners—Chesapeake Bay Region (Md. and Va.)—
History. I. Title. II. Series.
F187.C5B73   1988   975.5'18   87-46314
ISBN 0-8018-3677-8 (pbk.)

This time, for Amy.
Not just because she's my wife,
my love, and my friend,
but also because she knows first hand
what it's like out there.

RUN TO THE LEE

The third officer was surprised when he looked into his captain's eyes. They were moist as if he had been crying and his voice was strangely gentle when he finally spoke again. He held out the binoculars as if he were awarding a diploma.

—Take a good look, son. In some ways you aren't as lucky as I was. Take a good look and take your time . . . you may never see anything like her again.

From *Twilight for the Gods,* by Ernest K. Gann, William Sloane Associates, © 1956

CHAPTER

1

"It is hard for a sailor to believe that a boat
is an insensate thing of wood and metal:
you come to believe that it has its moods,
personality, and even a mind of its own."
From an article by Carleton Mitchell
in the *National Geographic Magazine*.

Do you ever look back fondly on your childhood and think
about how good it all was then? Does it ever seem to you that
things have never been so good as they were when you were
eight? Or nine? Or perhaps ten? Is there something that
seems to symbolize that wonderful past for you, some one
thing that stands out more than anything else when you
think of the things that made it the way it was?

For me there is.

Once upon a time there was a 90-foot schooner. Her name
was the *Albatross*. She sailed in the general cargo trade out of
Baltimore, and I don't suppose there is a river or deep water
creek south of the Patapsco where she wasn't known.

I only saw her twice in my life, so it's hard to believe she
could have become such a symbol to me until you consider
that I can't remember when I heard about her for the first

time. By the time I was five she had been the heroine of so many bedtime stories I couldn't begin to count them. I knew every member of her crew as a distinct personality although I had never seen any of them. The strength of her first mate was held up constantly as a reason for me to eat my spinach. In my mind I could see her, a great white sailboat, beautiful and majestic, a symbol of all that was good. And I felt that I knew her, although during all of that time I never actually saw her, but was seeing her through the eyes of someone else.

The *Albatross* was a two topsail schooner, rigged fore and aft. This may sound redundant, since all schooners are rigged fore and aft, but I use this term in reference to the topsails themselves. A topsail schooner, by definition, is a vessel of two or more masts, rigged fore and aft, carrying a square topsail and a topgallant sail on the foretopmast. Somehow, to me at least, this gives the impression that the designers started out to build a square-rigger, a brig, changed their minds about halfway down the foremast, and didn't bother to go back and change what they had already done.

The *Albatross* was not rigged in this manner. Her topsails were not square-rigged, but were set fore and aft, gaff topsails, fitting in between her masts and gaff-rigged mainsail and foresail like slices of pie. They were up there to fill a gap between two spars, where there was a wind to catch and a way to catch it. When they were furled they resembled shapeless sacks of something or other resting at the bases of the topmasts just where the jaws of the gaffs forked around the masts.

In spite of her aspiring name, she was a work boat, and no one, not even the most lubberly landlubber, would have ever confused her with a yacht or racing schooner. Her calling was there for all the world to see. It was evident in every sturdy line, every strong spar, and every inch of her stout rigging. It was there in an indescribable something about her that told the world that she earned her own way by hard labor and was proud of it. It was that same something you see in the faces of men who labor hard physically, do their work well, and are proud of it. There was nothing downtrodden or broken about her, nothing depressing or sick about the atmosphere that surrounded her. She was well cared for where it counted, but no effort was wasted to make her look like anything but what she was.

She always had a good coat of paint (although it was not always clean), any worn rigging was replaced instantly, and her sails, although patched in places, were strong and were never allowed to show frayed spots or the beginning signs of wear that come from stress around grommets and reef points. Her decks were kept reasonably clean, as clean as the load she was carrying would allow, and her brass always had a clear shine. She was hauled regularly and given a coat of fresh copper paint on her bottom, and each time she was hauled her planking was carefully inspected for evidence of worms.

In spite of her condition and her overall cleanliness, a close inspection left no doubt that she had carried coal, and a trip below decks and a sniff of her odors told that she had also carried tobacco, fish, molasses, and oysters. And no great effort was ever made to hide these odors. She had also carried coal oil, stoves, occasional odd shipments of household goods, fruit, vegetables, lumber, and at one time even a load of hogs. She was a work boat, and hauling cargo was her work.

From 1896 to 1918 my uncle was the owner and master of the *Albatross*, and the stories I heard were the stories of the time when he owned her, which was before I was born. He was really my great-uncle, although I called him Uncle John, and he was an old man by the time I came along and got to know him. He died when I was eleven, so I have little more than a small boy's memories and impressions of him. And I only saw the *Albatross* twice, both times when I was a youngster, once when she was at anchor and the other time under sail, but I've never forgotten either time, nor have I forgotten how differently I felt on each of those two occasions.

The first time I saw her was when I was ten, and was sailing as a cabin boy, brass-polisher, anchor-puller-upper, and general all-around privileged character aboard a 48-foot yawl named the *Natalie*. She was owned by my Uncle Tom, who really was my uncle, although he always treated me as if I were his favorite son.

We had come down the Bay, driving before a northeaster, coming out of the Choptank, changing course off Black Walnut Point, running free, boomed out, until we got to the mouth of the Patuxent. The Bay was dusty that day, and my grandfather, who was on the steamer, said he never thought we'd come out, and said afterward that he thought sure we were tied up in some snug little creek waiting it out. He may have said he thought it, and he may have hoped it, because his daughter was my aunt and she was aboard, but he was a smart man and he knew Uncle Tom, and I doubt if he really believed it.

Actually, there was nothing wild or risky about it. If there had been, Uncle Tom would have stayed in the Choptank another day. We weren't in any hurry. He was a good sailor, with about thirty years of Bay sailing behind him, and he wasn't a reckless man. But it was one of those good fall days, not long after Labor Day, when the weather settles down and there are times when the wind can haul down and blow northeast all day long and nothing kicks up. I can remember it as if it were yesterday, and I can recall that there wasn't a cloud in the sky from sun-up to sun-down. I know, because I saw the sun come up while I was catting the anchor in the Choptank, and I saw it go down over Solomons Island while I was fishing off the stern just inside Drum Point, although it was too windy and the fish weren't biting. They never bite much on a northeaster.

It blew, all right. It blew all day long. But it was a steady breeze, never varying a point, straight out of the northeast, the kind of breeze where you can steer a straight course, running before it wing and wing, without having to be on guard continually about jibing, and without having the jib flopping from one side to the other, filling, then collapsing, then filling again.

And of course the *Natalie* was a boat that could take care of herself in almost anything. She went down in the water a long way, and I don't know how much lead there was on the bottom of that fin, but I know it was considerable. She was stiff, I know that, and Uncle Tom always complained about that. He liked to carry a lot of water on the lee deck when he was beating to windward, and in the ten years he owned the *Natalie* he was never able to put her lee rail in the water and wash her deck, although he tore out two sets of chainplates before she convinced him.

But she could move, and she was easy to handle, and the breeze was steady that day. I can remember it because I had a two-hour trick at the wheel and it was a fast, easy trick. We didn't have a bit of trouble coming down, and we made it in a very short time.

We came into the mouth of the Patuxent, under the shelter of Drum Point, and dropped our hook close in shore, just

13

up river from a covey of two and three masters—schooners, pungys, and rams—that were waiting there, as they always did in those days, for the wind to ease and haul around to give them something other than a dead beat to windward going up the Bay.

After we had rounded up and dropped the hook, gotten the sails down and made them up, Uncle Tom took his glasses and started looking at the two master that was anchored nearest us. The tide was running flood and she was showing us her stern, and he looked at the name painted across her transom. "By God," he said. "I thought that was the old *Albatross,* and damn if it isn't."

I took the glasses and looked at her. I can remember that I wasn't very impressed, not after all I had heard about her. I felt disappointed and let down, as a matter of fact. Even then I couldn't remember the first time someone had told me about her, and over the years, until I saw her for that first time when I was ten, all kinds of images and fantasies built up in my little boy's brain about how she looked. But she didn't look like what I was seeing. I can remember the pain of feeling cheated.

I don't know why I had always pictured her in my mind as being a hard-gloss yacht white, since I certainly knew by that time that most of the work boats on the Chesapeake Bay were black, because they were easier to keep looking half-way decent if they were black. Except for the pungys, of course. For some reason they were painted a delicate shade of pink around the hull, "Pungy Pink" it was called, and the rails were painted watermelon green. Some of the rams were a faded whitewash sort of white going on gray, but the majority of them were black. In spite of knowing this, in the picture I had carried around in my mind she was white, sparkling white, and as I looked at her dull black hull I couldn't believe it was really the *Albatross.* Even the gold scrollwork around the border of her transom and the name plain as day didn't change my mind. This must be some other schooner named *Albatross.* This certainly wasn't the boat I had heard about all my life.

She was sitting low in the water, fully loaded with something, probably cantaloupes, I figured, it was that time of the year, and she looked squat and beamy to me, although I had never particularly noticed this characteristic before in all of the work boats I had seen. The curve of her hull from the waterline to gunwale, port and starboard, reminded me of a set of parentheses around a rather long word. I looked at the rest of the work boats anchored there, and sure enough, they were all pretty much the same. But in spite of this I had always thought of the *Albatross* as long and slender and sleek, my boyhood dreams completely ignoring her purpose in the economic scheme of things.

I looked at her masts, rising high above her broad deck, and then turned and looked carefully at the masts of the *Natalie,* studying their fine taper and graceful slenderness. Then I looked back at the *Albatross,* putting the binoculars to my eyes again, thinking of how much her masts looked like tall telephone poles, huge at the foot compared to those of the *Natalie,* and tapering very little, coming to an abrupt stop where they were overlapped by the topmasts. They were huge trees, skinned and shaped, but lacking the absolute smoothness and delicate workmanship of the *Natalie's* masts, and this was visible even from fifty yards away. They were like hand-hewn chair legs as compared to the ones turned out on a lathe, not perfect in their roundness, showing the flat spots left by the draw knife.

15

Her main boom was housed in a crutch on the after deck and the end of it was pointing directly at me, its diameter overwhelming me with its size. It was like everything else about her, big enough and strong enough not to have to worry about it giving way regardless of the weather, or so it seemed to me, a ten-year-old, a summer sailor, a boy who had never seen the Chesapeake Bay settle down and really get nasty. I wondered how Uncle John could have ever worried about rigging like that.

She could have gone right then, and it wouldn't have bothered her a bit, that long beat to windward, up to Baltimore, or wherever it was she was going. She wouldn't have even felt it, but her skipper, like all the rest of them anchored there that evening, figured the wind would go around to the southeast in the morning and she could crowd on her sail and run up the Bay in no time at all and it would be an easy passage for the crew. There wasn't much to hurry about in those days and there wasn't any point in beating the men down if it wasn't necessary. The cantaloupes or whatever it was would keep for another day.

"Able, isn't she?" Uncle Tom said when I put the glasses down on the wheel box.

I nodded, not looking at him, and I guess he must have seen what I was feeling. "Disappointed?"

I nodded again. "A little. I knew she was a work boat, skipper, but I didn't think she'd look so much like one."

"Well, she's a little run down since your Uncle John had her. But these are hard times for a sailboat that has to earn her own living, particularly here on the Bay. If you don't have the money to keep everything up to snuff you've got to do the best you can toward the most important things and let the rest of it go."

16

I didn't say anything more. I didn't want to tell him that I hadn't noticed that she was a little run down. Actually, I never did see a work boat that didn't look a little run down when you looked her over closely—times were hard for work boats when I came along—but I didn't say that either. I didn't say anything mainly because I didn't want to tell him I hadn't noticed it and that this wasn't the thing that was bothering me anyway. I didn't want to sound like the little boy I knew I was who had manufactured a dream and then had that dream exploded right in my face.

Uncle Tom was always pretty good to me, giving me a pretty free rein, letting me do what he thought I could do if there wasn't any reason why I shouldn't do it, and he knew I was dying to go over and row around her, so about an hour before supper he told me it would be all right if I wanted to go out rowing in the dink. He never called her a dinghy or a skiff. Dinghy was a little too fancy-sounding a term for him to use to describe a ten-foot rowboat, and when he spoke of a skiff he meant a rowboat with a flat bottom. The dink was round-bottomed and clinker-built.

The *Albatross* wasn't more than fifty yards away and it was only a short pull over there. I was there in a couple of minutes, rowing slowly up alongside her starboard quarter, about five yards away. As I pulled alongside, a man came up out of her after cabin, paused to look around, saw me in the dink, and walked to the quarter rail. He was smoking a pipe and was wearing a black turtle-neck sweater and a black cap with a small emblem on the peak. He rested both elbows on the railing and watched me. I was rowing slowly, pulling easily on one oar at a time, first the starboard, then the port, not really pulling, just dipping them and giving each a short jerk.

She was a little run down, I could see that. There was rust streaking down her black topsides just under her chainplates and she could have used a fresh coat of paint, although there weren't any bare spots showing. I could see parts of a large patch in her mainsail as it lay in the lazyjacks, and her trailboard scrollwork was peeling. There were places where the gilt lettering had disappeared. I didn't stop to think that I was comparing her to the *Natalie,* a pampered lady if ever there was one.

The man took the pipe out of his mouth and waved with the stem of it, without moving his elbows from the rail. "Good evening, Cap'n. Thinkin' of buyin' her?"

I smiled and shook my head. "Wish I could. Mighty able looking boat though, Cap'n."

"Could use a cabin boy. Like to sign on?" His voice was low, he hadn't raised it above a conversational level, but it carried out across the water.

"Already signed, sir," I replied, thinking suddenly of the last time someone had said that to me and I had said this to him. I had been rowing around that time too, just sightseeing in among the boats in the Washington Channel off the Capital Yacht Club, where Uncle Tom kept the *Natalie* between cruises. I had rowed up closeby to a large yacht moored just upstream from the *Natalie* and was looking her over when the door to her enclosed bridge opened and a man stepped out. He was wearing white flannel pants and a gray sweater. He waved, I waved back, and we talked about what a nice boat he had. I'll never forget how nice he was to me, and then he told me he could use a cabin boy. He smiled when he said it, and I knew even then that he didn't really mean it, but I thanked him and told him I already had a job. He asked me where, although I'm sure he knew, and I told him I was off the *Natalie*. "Well," he said, "if your Uncle Tom ever decides to sell her and you need a berth, you be sure to look me up."

When I got back to the *Natalie* I told Uncle Tom about it. He had a twinkle in his eyes and asked me which boat. I pointed her out. "Do you know who that man was?" he asked.

I shook my head.

"That was General Billy Mitchell, son. Sure you don't want to change your mind? I'll let you out of your contract if you want me to." But he was smiling when he said it too, and I knew that he didn't really mean it either. And it was all right, because I didn't want to, anyway.

I looked up into the rigging of the *Albatross*. I was pulling just hard enough to balance the tide. The man was still watching me. "What cargo are you carrying, sir?" I asked.

"Cantaloupes. Picked them up yesterday in Kinsale."

I couldn't think of any way to work it in without coming right out and saying it, so that's what I did. "My uncle used to own the *Albatross*."

"Your uncle? Who was that?"

"John Talbott," I answered. "He isn't really my uncle, but he is my great-uncle."

"John Talbott! He's your uncle?"

"Yes sir."

"Well, I'll be damned." He took his arms off the rail. "Would you like to come aboard, Cap'n?"

I hesitated, looking back at the *Natalie*, then shouted, "Hey, skipper!"

He was watching me and as I yelled he raised his arm and waved his hand up and out, which was our own hand signal for go ahead. It meant drop the anchor, raise the jigger, go about, cast off, and lots of other things too, but right now it meant it was all right for me to go aboard the *Albatross.*

I pulled alongside, and when I was close enough I turned the inboard oar flat, struck it smartly on the water, flexed my wrist, and lifted the oar handle, which lifted the entire oar, oarlock and all, pulled the oarlock out of its hole, and then set the oar and the oarlock down in the boat, being careful to wedge it in tightly between the top of the middle seat and the bottom of the stern seat so it wouldn't roll around or fall overboard. I didn't want this man to think Uncle John's great-nephew was a sloppy sailor.

I went forward and tossed up the painter, laying it across the rail just alongside him instead of hitting him in the face with it, and went back to ship the other oar. By the time I turned back he had passed the painter through a chock and made it fast to a deck cleat. I stepped up on the middle seat of the dink, grabbed the lower stanchion of her quarter rail, and put one foot up on the *Albatross'* rubbing strake. I climbed up and over the rail and dropped down onto the deck. He was smiling at me, and I knew he liked the way I had done it. "Somebody's sure raised you right, Cap'n," he said.

"Thank you sir. He's tryin' to."

"Who's he?"

"My Uncle Tom, sir. Over there on the *Natalie.*"

"I thought that was the *Natalie,*" he said. "I was below when you came in and I didn't see her name, but I was pretty sure. I've known your Uncle Tom for a long time, but it's been years since I've seen him. How is he?"

"He's fine, sir. Where did you know him?"

"Over in Cambridge. I had a skipjack over there that I used for oystering in the season. During the summer she laid around the dock tied up. He was working over there and he didn't have a boat, so one day late in April he came to see me. It was just about the end of the oystering season. He said he'd paint my boat and fix her up for the next season if he could have the use of her for the summer. I figured anybody like to sail that much oughta have something to sail, so I told him it was all right with me. He used her every summer he was there. I reckon it was about six years, all told."

"That must have been the *Bozman*," I said.

He nodded. "That's right. That was her name."

We were walking aft as we talked, walking toward the wheel. When we got there we stopped and turned around. I reached out and took the spokes of the wheel in my hands. I couldn't help it. I just had to do it. All my life I had heard about that wheel and I just had to know how it felt. I didn't move it, didn't make any effort to turn it, although I certainly wanted to. It was a big wheel, almost as tall as I was. I could barely see over the top of it. For a couple of minutes I stood there, wishing he would go away and not look at me. I wished he'd stop leaning against the wheel box and take a walk forward so I could be the captain of the *Albatross* and turn the wheel, give the orders, and make believe I was Uncle John coming down the Bay that night from Baltimore to Solomons Island in the snow.

We walked forward after that and he lifted a hatch cover to show me the cantaloupes in the hold. They were piled in up to the top and I don't think there was room for another one. The smell that came out of that hold was something wonderful.

I looked up at her rigging, following the lines of her stays, running my eye along the reach of her backstays down from the masthead to their fastenings on her rail. They were slack with no pressure on them, and they hung limply. I wondered how they sounded when they were stretched tight with the wind screaming through them.

We walked along the starboard rail, past a man working to loosen a stuck turnbuckle on one of her main shrouds. He looked around and smiled as we went by. We were talking about Uncle John and he was asking how he was and what he was doing. As we approached the companionway leading down into the forecastle a man came up the ladder. He paused as he stepped out on deck and looked at us. I heard the man beside me say, "Jack, this young man is Cap'n John Talbott's nephew. I'd appreciate it if you'd take him down and show him the foc'sle."

"Yes sir, Cap'n." He turned and smiled at me. "Watch your step a-goin' down that ladder. She's a steep one."

I went down and looked around. As soon as I got down I realized there was a man asleep in one of the bunks and I tried to be as quiet as possible as I moved around. The man the captain had called Jack didn't come all the way down, he just came as far as the bottom step, just far enough to have his head under the roof of the cabin trunk, and stood there watching me.

The skylight was open overhead and it was fairly light down there, but it got dark off in the corners. There wasn't much light coming in through the portholes. There wasn't much air stirring around down there either and there was a strong odor of stale sweat in the air. I stood and looked at the deck right at the base of the ladder for a long time, and then I looked up at the upper bunk on the starboard side. There were four bunks down there, upper and lower on either side. I reached up and ran my hand along the wood supports and along the smooth wooden sideboard of that top bunk. I felt

22

like I was touching history. I looked up at the man on the ladder. He was watching me, an interested smile on his face. I smiled back at him, not saying anything, and walked back to the ladder. He turned and went up on deck and I followed him.

The captain was waiting for us on deck and I followed him aft again, along the port side this time, the man he had called Jack going off down the starboard side, stopping where the man was working on the turnbuckle. I was still awed by the size of her. Ninety feet is a lot of schooner. I had expected to see more men, at least one more; Uncle John had a crew of four usually, and I knew from his clothes that the man sleeping forward was not part of the crew. "Where's the rest of the crew?" I asked.

"That's them. Me and a mate and one hand. Pretty good for these days. Boy asleep down forward ain't crew, he's just a farm boy I told I'd take to Baltimore on accounta his daddy's a friend of mine. Hard to get hands these days, not good hands, but any hands at all. All on the damn steamboats." He spit over the railing. "Either that or drivin' some damn truck. Cap'n Jimmy Hance told me the other day he came down the Bay last week just himself and one other man."

We went down through the after companionway and he opened the door to a cabin and stood back so I could go in. "This was your Uncle John's cabin. That desk over there was his. I don't think there's anything of his left in there though. I suppose he cleaned it out when he sold her, and I bought her from the man who bought her from him, and he cleaned it out too. But that was his desk, I know that."

I looked at the desk; it wasn't very big and it fastened to the bulkhead with a couple of door hooks, the kind you put on a screen door, with the screweyes in the frame. It was open and there were papers spread out on it. I remember that, and I remember seeing the log book in a little bookshelf over the bunk. There was a master's license framed on the wall next to the door and I walked over and read the name. "Toby M. Wheeler," it said.

I couldn't get over it for a minute. Just plain couldn't get over it. He was watching me, and I could see him smiling. I turned to him. "You were Uncle John's mate," I said, almost exploding.

He nodded. "You were on board that night," I said, the words tumbling out of my mouth. "You were, weren't you?"

He smiled. "I was on board that night. I surely was. And a lot of other nights too, but none like that one. I was on board."

I just stood there and looked at him.

"He was a hell of a man, that uncle of yours, he was one hell of a man. But I guess you already know that."

We walked back up on deck and I looked over at the *Natalie*. There was a towel tied in the rigging, on her jiggermast shrouds. That meant there's no hurry but when you see this come home. A blast on the foghorn meant drop what you're doing, whatever it is, and come now. I thanked him for showing me around, impatient now to get back to the *Natalie* and tell Uncle Tom all about what I had found. "Wish you didn't have to rush off," he said.

I pointed to the towel. "That means I'm wanted, sir. Maybe I can come over tomorrow morning before you leave to go up the Bay."

"Do that," he said. "Come over for breakfast. We'd all enjoy havin' Cap'n John's nephew for breakfast." He nodded his head. "Do that. And if we get a breeze and get out during the night, do it the next time. You're always welcome aboard the *Albatross,* Cap'n. And give my best wishes to your skipper. And don't forget to give my best to your Uncle John when you see him."

As I stood in the dink waiting for him to toss down the painter he told me to wait a minute, and walked over to the aft hatch cover. He lifted it, squatted down, and took several minutes selecting three cantaloupes from the cargo. He came back and handed them down to me. "Give these to your Uncle Tom. Tell him they ought to be just about right day after tomorrow."

The wind laid down during the night, and the next morning when I came up on deck there was a nice fresh breeze that had a lovely feel to it blowing into the mouth of the river out of the southeast. It was a breeze that had a lot of promise; give it a little time and it would build up to one of those long-roller breezes that will throw spray across the deck when you're going to windward. Right now, if you were beating into it, although that's hardly the word for it, you'd only hear a pat-pat-pat-pat against the hull. Each pat would be crisp and sharp, but there wouldn't be any spray coming over the side. With the *Natalie* you'd move right along feeling like you were drifting pretty fast, but you could leave a cup of coffee sitting on the wheel box and not spill a drop of it.

Uncle Tom was sitting in the cockpit when I came up on deck. He had his back against the edge of the cockpit and one foot up on the wheel box. He was crowning a new dinghy painter and I watched him for a couple of minutes, wondering if I'd ever be able to learn to crown a rope. I could do a good splice then, but no amount of practice seemed to do any good when it came to crowning.

I turned and looked down toward the lighthouse. All the boats were gone.

"They got an early start." He had looked up and seen me staring. "Breeze came up about five and they all got under way right soon afterward. Didn't you feel that breeze when it came up?"

I shook my head. "Didn't hear anything and didn't feel anything." I looked at the bridge clock. It said seven o'clock. It chimed six bells while I was looking at it. "They're well on their way by now," he continued. "Got themselves a fair wind and a flood tide."

She was gone and I hadn't had a chance to go over and say goodby. I didn't even get up early enough to watch her sail around the point. I felt pretty bad about it. I hadn't thought much about the possibility of the wind coming up so early. I had hoped it would hold off long enough so I could row over and have breakfast with them and say goodby before she left. I had changed my mind a little about her, and she didn't seem as ordinary as she had the day before. She wasn't the fanciful picture in a ten-year-old boy's imagination anymore, but she wasn't just any old work boat anchored behind Drum Point waiting for the wind to shift either. I had held the spokes of her big wheel in my hands, even though she wasn't under way, and I had walked her decks and looked down into her forecastle, seen that upper bunk on the starboard side that stuck in my mind—I don't know why that part of the story stood out so much—I had seen her crew, talked to some of them, and had even seen my Uncle John's cabin, where he had struggled that night to make a decision. And I had really met Toby Wheeler. That made her seem a lot different than she had first appeared through the binoculars.

I didn't see her again that summer. We went down the Bay

that day, down and around Point Lookout and into the mouth of the Potomac, spent the night in Smith's Creek, and started for home the next morning. Going up the river we spent the first night at Breton's Bay and the next night in Mattawoman Creek, and the next night I slept in my own bed at home for the first time since the middle of July. The bed rolled all night long, and I spent a restless, wakeful night. Once I woke up with my face turned toward the window. There was a large tree just outside and a branch of it hung down over the window. I opened my eyes, saw the branch just outside and above me, and leaped out of bed shouting, "We've gone aground!"

The next day I went back to school.

CHAPTER

2

"Ask every person if he's heard the story,
And tell it strong and clear if he has not."
From *Camelot,* by Lerner and Lowe.

ALL OF what I can remember about the Bay at that time is
what was seen through the eyes of a little boy between eight
and twelve years old. Most of what I know about the Bay
before that is what was heard through the ears of that same
little boy. Maybe that was what made it all seem so wonderful, but there were a great many other people who were older
than I who thought it was a pretty wonderful time to be alive
too. Maybe a lot of what I thought was so great was great
because it was shown to me—in a lot of cases downright
pointed out to me—by my Uncle Tom, who never got over
how wonderful it was to be on the water in a sailboat. When
I look back on it I think maybe he knew what was coming,
that we were reaching the end of an era, and he wanted
desperately for me to see it and know about it before it was
gone.

In the summer of 1937 he took me to Newport to watch
the America's Cup Races between the *Endeavour II* and the

Ranger. He took me that year, even though it meant skipping school for a week, but he wanted me to see it because he knew there would never again be anything like it. That was the end of an era too.

I came in on the tag end of an era, I suppose, and I don't really know first-hand what it was like in the early 1900's, when Uncle John was sailing the *Albatross,* but I think I know what it was like from all the stories I've heard, and the things I've read. I don't mean the things I've read in books, because it doesn't seem to me that there has been very much written about the Chesapeake Bay that grasped the flavor of that particular time, the way Mark Twain wrote about the Mississippi or Joel Chandler Harris wrote of Uncle Remus.

The reading I'm talking about is the old log books, the old tissue paper manifests from the wharfs along the rivers, stories in the newspapers that were current news—written the way the people talked then, with the values people had then —an old diary, and the company instructions to the captains and pursers of the line explaining the company procedures and regulations. And even these things wouldn't mean so much or be read with such reverence if it weren't for all those stories I heard as a boy; I have known a lot of people who lived through those times, and when they talked I listened, and I remember a great many things they said, and most of all I remember their tone of voice.

And I saw some of it, and a certain amount of it rubbed off from my Uncle Jimmy, who wasn't my uncle either, but like my Uncle John was my great-uncle. I guess I saw the parts of it that were good enough to hold on until the very last, until the crash of 1929 and the Depression that really ended all of it. Maybe I don't remember it the way it really was, and maybe my thoughts are colored because they are the memo-

29

ries of the thoughts of a small boy, like the way I pictured the *Albatross* until I actually saw her, but it seems to me that there never has been a time when things seemed so good. Things changed back then, but they changed very slowly, and unless you looked a long way back over your shoulder you didn't even realize they were changing.

Uncle John bought the *Albatross* in 1896, and she was still sailing in 1929, and may be sailing somewhere in this world even today for all I know, because there are some places in the world where things still change very slowly and sailboats still carry cargo and earn their keep. There are still sailboats hauling cargo in the East and West Indies, and in the Indian Ocean. From the time he bought her until the time he sold her she did exactly the same thing she was doing when he bought her, and when I saw her in 1929, eleven years after he sold her and the same year he died, she was still doing the same thing.

Nothing changed no matter who had her, and I imagine she had the same problems of earning her living all her life, and maybe still does, even today. She came along, fresh and new, about the time steam was showing its muscle on the Bay, and she fought all her life against the steamboats, and in the end, when the trucks and good roads were slowly strangling the steamboats, she was still out there fighting and holding her own. When the Depression came along and suddenly ended the agony of the steamboats, she was still around doing her job. I didn't see her doing it, but I saw some of her sisters, and I knew she was around someplace.

The geography of the Chesapeake Bay brought her into being and kept her alive. It furnished her means of livelihood for years, as it did for all water traffic, for there was a time when almost everybody lived along the rivers and creeks,

30

much the same way almost everybody lives along the highways and streets today. The rivers and creeks were the highways and streets of those times, and everything the people had came to them in a boat, and everything they shipped off to market went in a boat, and when they traveled they went in a boat usually.

But it was tough on the Bay for a sailboat. There was always the steamboat, with her published timetable, her lack of dependence on the wind, and her ability to thumb her nose at the weather and go while the sailboats were either tied up in some harbor or becalmed in the middle of the Bay. It was seldom that a schooner captain looked around without seeing at least one smudge of black smoke on the horizon to remind him of his constant struggle with progress.

But things changed very slowly back then, and most of the men who sailed the Bay, both in steam and under canvas, didn't realize that progress was stalking them from over the hills as the State improved its highways and General Motors and Freuhauf improved their trucks and trailers. In the booming economy of the twenties there was enough for all, including the few trucks that were already on the highways. The watermen seldom went back into the countryside, and thus they saw little of the road building that was to change their lives, except for the last mile or two that led down to the wharf; but when it came, the Depression came to all of them, all at once. And when things got better, the boats were gone and the trucks had stepped in to fill the gap. When the economy began to move again the watermen looked back at the docks and found them rotted, looked back for the steamers and found them gone.

Only a few of the schooners remained. They were made of tougher material, or maybe it was the men who sailed them

31

to the bitter end, refusing to go ashore, refusing to give up their way of life as long as the slightest chance remained.

They were a tough breed, those Bay schooner captains. They usually owned their own boats and lived pretty much by their own wits. They could smell a cargo that was over the horizon and up a creek, sense a squall in their joints long before the glass dropped even slightly, and feel their way around the Bay in bad weather by pure instinct, aided a little, of course, by the feel of the wind on their sensitive earlobes and perhaps a taste of mud from the bottom. Most of them could have held their own with any clipper captain who ever sailed down the Patapsco for the Horn.

Today, like the schooners they sailed, they are only a memory. They were men like my Uncle Jimmy, who started under sail and went to steam early in his life, and my Uncle John, who resisted for a while, then couldn't refuse when the course of events put it to him in 1918. He was offered command of a Bay steamer, at a salary he was not able to refuse since he had two sons who wanted to be doctors. But this didn't change his opinion. Every time he passed a sailboat beating her way to windward he would leave the pilot house and step out on the bridge to watch her slide past and drop astern. There was always envy in his eyes at times like that— envy for the man who stood at her wheel feeling that he was the master of a living thing with a mind of her own, and homesickness for the closeness of the spray crashing over the bow and creaming along the lee rail. I knew him and remember him during those last few years before he retired, and the few years after that until he died, and many a time I watched him spit carefully to leeward with great deliberation when the word steam was mentioned.

During those retirement years, as he lived out his life on a

32

farm overlooking the river that had been his boyhood play-
ground, he talked a great deal to me about his life as a boy,
using incidents in his life rather than theoretical lectures to
show me life's values. With the typical curiosity and inquisi-
tiveness of a small boy, I assailed him with questions about
the old days, about his boyhood, and about the *Albatross*. I
was awed by his age, the fact that he was even older than my
father, and there were times when I know he must have been
shaking with silent laughter as I asked him about events that
must have occurred sometime near the voyage of Columbus. I
expected his comments to be those of an on-the-spot observer,
and why not? He must have been there.

I can remember distinctly asking him about the battle between the *Bon Homme Richard* and the *Serapis*. John Paul
Jones was one of his heroes, and thus one of mine, and when
he had finished a graphic story of the battle, I asked him how
many Britishers he had killed that day.

Uncle John was born in 1862 in a farmhouse on an arm of
land at the mouth of St. Leonard Creek in Calvert County,
Maryland. This creek opens on the Patuxent River and is
without question the most beautiful creek along its entire
length. On the day he was born his father, a Confederate
soldier, was a prisoner in a Union prison less than a hundred
miles away. Uncle John's family, like many of their neighbors
in Southern Maryland, were Southern sympathizers, but the
state in which they lived did not leave the Union.

When Richard Talbott went south to join the Confederate
Cause he did not take his wife because of the short time until
the birth of his son. He was taken prisoner at the battle of
Seven Pines as the Union Army moved on Richmond, and
was shipped to the Union prison at Point Lookout. He never
saw his son, even though he was in the same state and on the

33

same side of the battle line. Ellen Talbott took her little son to the prison only once and was denied permission to see her husband and show him their son. She did not go again. Her husband died in 1864 of dysentery and various associated causes, such as malnutrition, exposure, and pneumonia.

Ellen Talbott, caught up in all of the bitterness and hatred of life in a border state, not knowing for months that her husband was dead, not knowing in fact until one of the returning prisoners told her, never knowing where his body was buried, faced with the prospect of running a large farm without a husband, faced with the prospect of raising a small, fatherless boy, knowing well who were her friends in the community, and knowing also those who hated her as a rebel sympathizer, squared her shoulders and continued to run the farm as she had done during the years her husband was in prison.

Only her outlook changed. Until the day she learned that Richard Talbott was dead, she had run it for the day when he would return and she could go back to being the wife of a gentleman farmer. She had never considered the possibility of leaving her native state to move to Virginia or into the Carolinas. She had never thought the Union would fail, had never really wanted it to fail, although she had hoped at first that the Southern victories would bring some compromise short of total victory and secession. After Gettysburg and Vicksburg she hoped the Southern forces could hold on and force some compromise short of total defeat. After Richmond fell she held the farm in a grimly determined way, knowing her husband would need something to which he could return after the final defeat.

Her purpose in life changed the day Teddy Parker came

34

shuffling up the road, limping slightly, a gaunt reminder of defeat, a shadow of the handsome, well-fed young man who had told of his decision to go South with her husband four years before on the Talbott front porch.

That night, as Ellen Talbott put her young son to bed, she was still numb from the news. Although there had been times during the evening when she had been on the verge of tears, and would have welcomed the release they would have brought, she was still dry-eyed. The moment for tears, the moment of hearing the awful words, had seen her rush to comfort Teddy, who went completely to pieces and became almost hysterical.

Later, when the house was silent and the servants had gone to bed, she slowly climbed the steps and went to her room. She knew that she no longer needed to watch the creek and the road for her husband. He would never come. There was no doubt about it. She stood in the middle of the room and looked at the bed. She had slept in it alone for many nights and she knew she would probably sleep alone in it for the rest of her life. The only things she had left were the farm and her son. She could sell the farm and move to the city to do she knew not what, or she could stay and continue to do what she had been doing. Eventually she decided to keep the farm and do her best to give her son the kind of life he would have had if his father had come home from the war, or at least give him the same peace and quiet, the same room to grow, and the freedom to roam.

Uncle John grew up on that farm, close to the water and always influenced by its presence, and at an early age he began to learn to take care of himself in a boat. By the time he was six he had learned to swim—his mother saw to that—and he was going with "Uncle" Fred and his son Ned on crabbing and fishing trips in the sheltered creek. When he was eight he was rowing out on his own, into the mouth of the creek, to catch fish for the table.

Soon he was crabbing along the shore for hard crabs and picking soft crabs out of the nearby marshy grass that grew in the spots where mud washed down into the creek, supplying all that could possibly be used for the table, taking the rest for fishbait.

During the lazy summer days when the fish weren't biting, he and Ned would take the skiff and play steamboat up and down the creek, pretending that each point was a landing, loading and unloading imaginary cargo.

His mother made little effort to turn his interest away from the water and toward the land. But she required that certain chores be done before he could devote himself solely to amusement. The crabbing and fishing were never treated as entertainment or recreation; they were his duties, the providing of food for the table. The care of the boats, the skiff and tonging canoe, was his chore, and as he grew older his responsibility extended from simply keeping the boats bailed and dry to painting, caulking, and general repair. Ellen Talbott always insisted that he have a definite plan for all of his actions, a plan that he had thought out and that took into account all eventualities.

When he and Uncle Fred hauled the boats in the spring to overhaul them, she insisted that they know what materials they were going to need and have everything on hand down on the shore, instead of running back and forth to the shed or having to put the work aside while they ordered something sent down from Baltimore on the steamer. Thus as a young man Uncle John fell into the habit of doing everything with careful planning and an awareness of possible problems that might arise. However, there was nothing dull or methodical about him, nothing plodding. He always found his mother ready to help him with any project that made sense, not necessarily to her, but to him, and she actively encouraged him to question and seek knowledge in all directions.

When he was thirteen he went to his mother after dinner one night and laid out on the table a thorough set of plans for a sailing skiff, one of his own design, and asked her if he could build it. Ellen Talbott knew very little about sailboats, but she liked the thorough way he had gone about it, and told him she would take the plans over to the wharf in the morning when the steamer came in and ask Uncle Mason, who was the captain, if he thought it was a good design. When Uncle Mason approved the plans and added that he thought they were extremely well drawn, she told him to go ahead. She even helped him design and make the sails for the boat, working alongside him with palm and needle. When the 16-foot skiff was finished and hauled to the water's edge she was the one who launched it, breaking a small bottle of her own grape wine across its bow. And once it was in the water and rigged, she was the first passenger.

In the fall and early winter, and then again in the spring, he went with Uncle Fred in the larger boat out into the river to the oyster beds and culled the oysters that the man threw up onto the culling board. When he was fourteen he was using a set of tongs himself, working alongside Uncle Fred and Ned, who was about his own age. Between the three of them they could bring up a good mess of oysters in less time than it took to sail out and back.

The oyster boat was a twenty-two foot tonging canoe, a sloop-rigged double-ender with a long, narrow cockpit with a high collar around it. She steered with a long, gracefully curved hickory tiller that ran from her cockpit back to the very point of her stern where it slipped over the post of a rudder that curved down and out, away from the sternpost, until it reached the waterline. Her mast, which was large and sturdy and stood without stays, was twenty-six feet tall, somewhat taller than the usual, and the day arrived when that mast became a symbol to John Talbott of the day he attained true manhood.

The day was cold and windy. John Talbott was sixteen. It was the middle of December and the temperature was low and the humidity high. A northeaster had settled in, bringing low clouds, rain, and winds of ten to fifteen miles an hour. The rain was falling out of clouds no more than two hundred feet above the ground, and where it fell on a tree limb or a gate post it froze. Occasionally a gust of wind would rattle the windows in the house, and upstairs it was cold and damp. John was glad when he finished dressing and could leave the chill of his room to come downstairs into the warmth of the breakfast room where he ate with his mother before a roaring open fire.

Shortly after breakfast Ellen Talbott sent for Uncle Fred. When he arrived she told him she wanted him to take John and Ned and get her about six bushels of oysters to send to Baltimore on the steamer in the morning. Uncle Fred gazed out the window with a pained expression on his face, looking at the rain, the entire time she spoke.

"It is the least we can do," she told John after Uncle Fred left dejectedly to find his son. "We had a bad crop last year because of the drought and we didn't make enough to be able to go to Baltimore and do any Christmas shopping. But we are not going to let Christmas pass without sending presents. We will send everybody a quart of oysters and a side of bacon. We will wrap them in fancy paper, and at least they will know we are thinking of them."

"But Mother," John said, "can't we wait a couple of days? Maybe we'll get a break in the weather. It's raining and blowing out there and that rain is freezing. Look at it on that porch railing out there."

"I know it is, son, but we can't wait. The steamer is coming in tomorrow morning and we'll have to have them wrapped and ready to give to your Uncle Mason. Next time will be too late. I know it is a bad day for it, but you just do what Uncle Fred says and everything will be all right. I'll have something hot for you all to drink when you come in."

He went up to his room, dressed himself in his warmest clothing, and pulled on his oilskins overtop. He went downstairs and out onto the porch, sat down on the wooden bench, and pulled on his boots. As he got up and walked to the edge of the porch he saw Uncle Fred and Ned come walking around the house, both dressed in their oilskins. He greeted them with a shrug. "I tried," he said. "But she said go."

"Ah knowed she would," Uncle Fred replied. "Miss Ellie, she a mighty strong lady when she make up her min' to be. Well, I reckon we better git on out there. Them oysters is a-waitin'."

The tonging skiff was well down in the water, wallowing in the light swells in the creek. The water was up above her floorboards. They pulled her alongside the wharf and John and Ned stepped gingerly down on her bow and stern, balancing themselves carefully. Soon they had bailed her down to a point where the water was below the floorboards. Uncle Fred came aboard and began to work on the frozen knots of the sail stops that held the sails furled. He finished freeing them at about the same time there was only an inch of water

39

in close to the centerboard well. "All right," he said. "That's good, boys. Let's git the sails on her."

The canvas was cold and wet and stiff. It was hard to handle but they hauled the head of the mainsail to the masthead, set the jib, and ran before the wind down the creek and out into the open water. It was quiet except for the sound of the rain hitting the water.

They rounded the point and slid along the shore, easing out into the river under the shelter of the high banks along the shoreline. The water was fairly smooth but they could feel the push of the wind on the top of the mainsail. The wind was jumping off the bank and sometimes striking the surface of the water, but its main force was fifteen feet overhead. The water was slightly choppy and as they moved further out into the river they began to feel the full force of the wind. As they passed the oyster stakes that marked the inner edge of the oyster bar they were in open water, out from under the lee of the hills.

Uncle Fred, who was at the tiller, swung the boat around into the wind, Ned dropped the anchor, and the boat swung into the tide when the sails came down. She lay broadside to the wind and waves, bow up the river in the ebb tide, and rocked back and forth as the men worked silently and quickly.

The oyster bar they were working over was a natural growth about two hundred yards off shore. The bed was not worked commercially. Its only purpose was to supply oysters for the Talbott table, and its oysters were allowed to grow to good size before they were taken.

The only problem the bed presented was its reputation. It was known far and wide as the place where the best oysters in the river grew. For a short time Ellen Talbott had her troubles with poachers. She knew who they were, the shiftless sons of a shiftless family who lived several miles down the river. They would come up the river in the early morning when the fog blanketed the water, following the shoreline just at dawn, and after they passed the mouth of the creek they would turn out into the river to the bed. In the stillness of a foggy morning they could be heard working out there. The sound of their tongs, the sound of the oysters falling on the culling board, and the splash of the culls falling back into the water could be clearly heard on the bank in front of the house.

One morning John looked out the window and saw his mother walking out on the bank. He had heard the door slam and gone to the window. He was somewhat startled to see his mother carrying a rifle. He raised the window and leaned out as she reached the edge. She stopped, stood and listened for a minute, and then leaned the rifle against a tree and put her hands to her mouth. "Harry Long! Harry Long! I can hear you out there, Harry Long! I know you're out there, Harry Long! I can't see you, but I know you're out there!"

John could hear the sound of oysters falling on the culling board. "I've got a rifle here, Harry Long! I can't see you, but I am going to start shooting!" She picked up the rifle. John could still hear the sound of oystering drift in off the water. BANG! After the echo stilled he listened and heard nothing. Then he heard the sound of oars creaking in oarlocks, and creaking very rapidly, he noticed. BANG!

Then he heard a shout from out in the fog. "We're goin'! We're goin'!"

His mother turned and walked toward the house. John saw a look of absolute triumph on her face. "Maybe that will teach them," he called down.

41

She looked up at him and smiled. "A lesson they certainly can use. Maybe I will get one of them if they come back again."

But this day there was no one else out there on the oyster bed. In fact, they could see no other boats anywhere on the river. When the culling board, laid across the cockpit, was filled, Uncle Fred turned to Ned. "All right there, boy. Now you stop tongin' for a while and cull them oysters. Let's see if you can't fill a couple of them bushel baskets with what you got there."

The rain had eased off to not much more than a fine mist by the time they were finished, but the wind, just overhead, was blowing even harder, and they were sure it was colder than it had been when they came out. "I spec' that's enough to satisfy youah momma, John. I spec' we can get on in now. Let's git the sail on her and go home."

Ned went forward and began to pull on the main halyard. It didn't move. Uncle Fred rolled his eyes up toward the top of the mast. "Pull it agin, boy. What's the matter with you, you tuckered out?"

"Ah ain't tuckered out. That block up theah she froze up."

"Heah, lemme try it, son."

Uncle Fred pulled on the halyard, jerked it a couple of times, then pulled on it again. "She froze up all right. Right on to that block up theah."

John was watching the top of the mast, hoping for even the slightest movement. He saw none. He looked down at the others, standing by the mast, the halyard dangling in their hands. They were both looking at him. He looked back up at the masthead, slowly, deliberately, just as if it wasn't cold and they had all day. No one spoke. He waited. Then he looked out across the water to the mouth of the creek. There was

42

only one oar in the boat, a long, sculling sweep, and he doubted if anyone of them could scull the heavy boat up into the mouth of the creek against the wind and the ebb tide, now running full.

He looked back at the others. Uncle Fred was looking at the oar in the bottom of the boat. John slowly shook his head. "We can't scull her against that tide and wind. There's only one thing to do. One of us has to shinny up that mast and free that block."

They were still looking at him. Neither of them looked at the other. The boat seemed to be rocking even more now, and as John looked up again the masthead seemed to be traveling a much wider arc than it had before.

He gave one last look at the masthead, then turned, bent over, and ran his hand along under the deck until it touched an oyster knife that was sticking into one of her deck timbers. He pulled it out. It had a hole in the handle and a loop of twine through it large enough to fit over his wrist. He walked forward to the mast, reached up as far as he could, feeling suddenly exhilarated, took the mast in his hands, wrapped his legs around, and began to pull himself slowly upward. The mast was wet and slippery, but he made good progress up to about fifteen feet above the deck. It was there that he came into contact with the first of the ice.

He took a tight grip with his legs, reached out with one hand and grabbed the main halyard. He began again to work his way up the mast, using the halyard to steady himself while he felt up the mast to get himself a good grip. Slowly he worked his way toward the peak, feeling the swing of the mast increase with each foot he climbed. Once he turned and looked over his shoulder to shout to the deck, then turned back quickly and laid his face against the cold of the mast. He

43

had been looking straight down into the icy water at the very end of one of the swings of the mast.

Gradually he felt the ice of the windward side of the mast begin to penetrate his oilskins and warm clothing. From his crotch to his neck he felt a solid line of almost unbearable cold begin to go deeper and deeper into his body.

Finally he reached the peak. He held on with his left hand, wrapped tightly around the mast, reached down and behind him with his right hand, caught the two lines of the halyard, brought them around under his legs and lifted them, then looped them into a clove hitch around the top of the mast, resting the full weight of his body on one of them, allowing the other to hang slightly slack, thus bringing his body weight to bear on the frozen block. In this way he made himself a sort of bosun's chair, and felt more secure than before. Nevertheless, he still held on with his left hand and worked with his right, remembering the age-old saying of topmast hands. "One hand for the ship and one for yourself."

The boat was still rolling back and forth and he wondered how far he was swinging through the air with every whip of the mast. The frigidness of the mast was penetrating even further into his guts. His hands were growing numb and he found it difficult to make his fingers do what he wanted them to do as he hacked away at the ice in the block with the oyster knife, trying not to damage the halyard as he did it.

The entire lead through the block was filled with ice. He picked at it, chipping a little at a time, missing sometimes as the movements of the boat caught him off balance, feeling his strength ebbing away with each movement as the cold penetrated his body. He was frightened to find himself growing drowsy. He knew this was a danger sign and a perilous thing

44

to have happen at the top of the mast. He tried shouting back and forth to the men on the deck, but soon gave this up as too much work and not really very important. For a few moments he didn't really care if he went to sleep or not. He shouted aloud each time he swung the knife. He started counting the number of times he picked away at the block. He stopped counting at twenty-five. It wasn't doing much good. He was going to sleep anyway. He felt his eyelids growing heavier in spite of everything he did. He really didn't care very much. It wasn't so important after all. They could spend the day and night out there, if necessary. Someone would come out and get them after a while anyway. He would just take a nap up there and wait for someone to come. It wasn't so damn important to get that block free after all.

All the time he was chipping away at the pulley. He was missing now more times than he was hitting. Each time it was an effort to raise his arm again. He swung at the block one more time, figuring this would be the last time he could do it. He would just wrap his arms around the mast and go to sleep for a while. And if he fell off the mast, well, he really didn't care too much about that. He felt the impact of the point of his knife as it hit the ice in the block. He felt it in his shoulder bone, wondering why he felt nothing in between. Suddenly, he fell.

Jolted out of his stupor, he clung to the mast, realizing after a second or two that he had only dropped a couple of inches as the rope broke free from the block and the two parts of the halyard equalized themselves. But the rope was free, and that knowledge ended the lethargy he had felt. He summoned all of his strength, raised himself off the halyard, unwound the clove hitch and let the halyard fall free. He slid down the mast, feeling nothing but a dull impact in his hip

45

joints as his feet hit the deck. With the greatest physical effort he steadied himself, consciously fighting to keep from lurching or staggering, and stepped down into the cockpit to return the oyster knife to its place in the deck timber. He took the tiller in his hand, closing his fingers around it with great effort. "All right, Fred. Raise the mainsail before the damn thing freezes again. Ned, get up the anchor. Let's go home."

Fred looked at him, his face aglow with admiration. "Yes suh, Mr. John, yes suh!"

When they got ashore and got back to the house Ellen Talbott gave them each a cup of hot tea. John took his cup into the breakfast room, pulled a chair up in front of the fire and sat, cradling his cup in the palms of his hands, staring into the fire. He was vaguely aware of voices in the kitchen.

His mother came in a few minutes later holding a steaming mug. She took the teacup out of his hands, replacing it with the mug. "As long as you know how to act like a man you might as well have a man's drink," she said.

He looked up at her, little expression on his face, his eyes still almost blank.

"It's hot buttered rum," she said. "Don't drink it all at once."

When he began to warm up a little she came and sat beside him. For a long time she said nothing. Finally she cleared her throat. He turned and looked at her. "I'm proud of you, son," she said. "That took a tremendous amount of courage. And a great deal of determination as well."

He took a sip of the rum. "I was lucky I didn't fall off that mast and break my neck," he said with a grunt.

"Son," she said, "don't ever trust anything so flimsy as luck." She put her hand lightly on his forearm. "There is no amount of bad luck that can't be defeated by persistence and

46

courage, and no amount of good luck that can't be defeated by half-heartedness and lack of planning. I am a good deal older than you are, son, and I have learned to leave nothing to luck or chance and I've tried to teach you the same thing. If there is anything I have tried to teach you it is that. I really don't think such a thing as luck even exists."

"I wonder how long I was up on that mast?" he asked idly.

"Uncle Fred says it was about a half an hour."

He shook his head. "Seemed like all day. Oysters! I'll never eat another one as long as I live. I hate those damn things."

After that, when they went out in the tonging skiff, John did the sailing, gave the orders, and handled the tiller.

In 1881, when John Talbott was nineteen, he left on the steamer for Annapolis to attend St. John's College. While he was there he worked diligently, leaving nothing to luck as was the habit of some of his classmates, and was graduated *summa cum laude*. The following year, after a summer at home on the water, he went to Baltimore to become a law clerk in the office of his mother's brother, Henry Thomas. He planned to stay there long enough to acquire enough knowledge to pass the bar examination and then return to practice law in his home county.

In November of that year, 1886, he received a message that dashed his dreams. One of the men off the *St. Marys* came to his room near the law office and told him that his Uncle Mason said he was to pack and come to the boat immediately. His mother had been taken seriously ill and he was to come home immediately. He would be needed to run the farm until she recovered.

In spite of having grown up on the farm, he knew very

little about how to run it, or how it ran. His mother had always made the decisions, kept the books, hired and fired, and decided on what crops to plant where. She had been in complete charge. His earliest memory of her was the daily ritual that always took place just before he went to bed. She would unlock the pantry and measure out the supplies for the next morning's breakfast. So much coffee, so much flour, so much sugar, and so many eggs.

She had never wanted John to be a farmer as such, only a land-owner, and had heartily approved of his decision to go into the practice of law. She had wanted him to grow up with the free run of the place, go to school, get his degree, become a lawyer, and then return home. There was time enough after he came back a lawyer to learn what was necessary about running a farm.

As he came down the Bay on the steamer he found himself wondering how he would be able to manage the place. He knew almost nothing about it except that it bordered on a creek that opened out into the river. When he got up in the morning he looked out at the creek and down the river, never back at the rolling acres of the farm. His entire boyhood life was centered around the creek and the river. His mother had let him have his childhood, knowing the time would come soon enough for him to face the responsibility of manhood.

When the boat docked he came ashore and handed his baggage down into the rowboat tied along the side of the wharf close inshore. "How is she, Fred?" he asked, as the man took the luggage.

Fred shook his head. "She ain't doin' so good, Mr. John."

"What's wrong with her? Uncle Mason didn't know. He just said come home."

48

"She's got the typhoid, Mr. John." His voice was soft, as if he were talking to himself.

"Typhoid!"

"Yes suh, typhoid fever."

"How in the hell could she have gotten typhoid fever?"

"Ah don' know, suh, but the doctor, he say,—heah, gimme youah han' and let me hep you down—the doctor he say she mussa been drinkin' some bad water someplace. Mussa been someplace 'sides ouah place. We ain't never had no bad water outa that well. You know that for a fac'."

"Well, what does the doctor say, Fred? What does he say?"

"He don' say nothin' to me, Mr. John. He jes come and go and look mighty worried, but he don' say nothin' to me."

John approached his mother's room with a heavy heart. He knew about typhoid fever. He knew that very few people ever recovered from typhoid fever. As he came up the steps and turned toward the door it opened and the doctor came out. He looked at John and there was something in his expression that made John know he had gotten there too late.

"She's dead?"

The doctor nodded. "I'm sorry, son. I knew you were coming and I did all I could, but—well, there wasn't much I could do."

After the funeral, John unpacked and settled in. He knew he would not be going back to Baltimore to read law. He was needed too badly on the farm.

From 1886 to 1894 John Talbott ran the farm his mother had left him, but always with his head turned, looking over his shoulder toward the water. He read law in Prince Frederick and passed the bar examination in 1888, but he felt no strong attachment to his small law practice, his home, or his farm—only the water that lay around it. If it hadn't been for

49

the people on the farm who were depending on him to give them the guidance and help they needed, he would have thrown the whole thing up and left shortly after his mother's death. Without her there it was no longer like home. Many times, stealing an hour or two after dinner in the summer when the days were long, he would sail out to the best spot he knew and fish the turn of the tide.

The vista as the river opened up toward Point Patience was one that stirred and disturbed him. It tempted him. He wondered about the possibilities of selling out and going to sea. He had some experience. He had spent the summers between his college terms as a quartermaster on the *St. Marys*, and knew he could ship out as an officer on a steamer. Uncle Mason would see to that. But there was the farm, the little colony of people who lived there and counted on him. What would happen to them if he left?

In the summer of 1894 the problem solved itself. He met a man on the boat coming down from Baltimore who was coming into the area to acquire a farm. John had gone up to see his crop sold, sick at the price it brought that year—it seemed to him that it had been a lot of sweat over nothing—and as he sat at dinner he talked to the man next to him. They got off the boat together and the next morning the sale was completed. John felt that he had studied the man and knew his people would be well taken care of. He also knew that this man was not going to grub a living out of the earth but was intending to savor the peace and quiet of the beautiful countryside as a country gentleman with an outside income could.

Once the arrangements were made and the money deposited in a bank account in Baltimore, John went about the business of packing up the things he wanted to keep, those things that had meant so much to his mother, and the things that seemed valuable. He had everything packed and crated and shipped to Baltimore on the steamer. With a minimum of furniture in the house, he waited for the new owner to come down and take possession. The steamer would drop him off on the way up the river and pick John up on the way back down. And then he would go to Baltimore and start his new career on the water. That was the way he planned it and it might have happened that way had it not been for the arrival of the *Albatross* in the creek on the evening before the steamer was due.

He was sitting on the front steps after supper, his back against a pillar, looking down the river. It was a clear, warm evening, and there was a gentle, whisper of a breeze out of the east-south-east. She was coming up the river, coming toward him almost bows-on, ghosting along, a ripple at her bow, her sails drawing nicely in the light breeze.

He watched her work her way past the point and glide into the entrance of the creek. He had never seen anything like her before, and all interest in steamboats died at the sight of her. She was new, or almost new at that time, her hull was freshly painted, and there wasn't a patch on her sails. She was a magnificent sight coming into the creek, and the minute she was at the wharf he was in the rowboat, pulling across the creek.

The money stayed in the bank in Baltimore for two years. And then he drew out sufficient of it to buy the *Albatross* for his own. In those two years he had learned all there was to know about her, all there was to be taught about how to make her pay. Her skipper had taken him on board as first mate, knowing his ambition, and seeing instantly the answer to a problem. The problem was to find someone who would buy the *Albatross* in two years, buy her and love her, and

51

treat her the way she was entitled to be treated. For the *Albatross* was the realization of a dream to her skipper. He was sixty-eight years old, and he had owned her four years, sailing her out of Newport News, seldom reaching this far up the Bay. She represented everything he had in life, all that he had been able to save as a deckhand, mate, captain, and owner of a smaller, older, less seaworthy boat. All of this he had put together four years previously and commissioned a yard in Newport News to build her. She was his own design, and she was fast, seaworthy, and beautiful.

In 1896 Uncle John bought her, as he had said he would, and he sailed her until 1918. By then it was touch and go. He wasn't losing money, but he was just making a comfortable living with nothing left over to go into the savings account. He could see the day coming when she would cost him, so he sold her and went aboard the steamer to round out his career, retiring in 1927. The sale of the *Albatross* assured the medical school tuition of his two sons, and when Richard went into practice two years after Jack hung out his shingle, and the two formed a partnership, he figured the sacrifice was well made.

He never told me much about his days on the steamboat, but he always had a story to tell me about the *Albatross*, and like all children I had my favorite, and I never heard it too many times. I'd ask for it over and over again, and although I had heard it before, I remember it best the way he told it one warm spring Sunday as we sat on the front porch and watched the steamer come down the river, pass Swanson's Point, pass the red spar off Town Point, and make the turn for the wharf at Benedict.

He was sitting in his rocking chair there on the front porch. It was a green chair with a caned seat and back, with wide arms, and each arm had a knob about the size of a half a dollar up where you rested your hands. I never did know what they were for. He was watching the boat and we were waiting for her to blow her whistle. No railroad engine, not even the Duquesne Limited running wide open, ever had a whistle that sounded like the one on the *Anne Arundel*.

He was an old man then, and I can remember the purple splotches on the backs of his hands, the way the veins stood out, and the way his skin looked fine like parchment. But he was still strong, alert, and vigorous, not like he was trying to prove anything, but that's just the way he was. He was not spry and bright in the manner of some old people who attempt to convince themselves and others that they are not allowing their age to slow them down, thus losing the dignity and nobleness that comes with accepted age. He could spin out a yarn at a moment's notice when he found a receptive audience, which I always was. There was nothing vague or meandering about his stories, as there is with some old people when they speak of half-forgotten memories, debate with themselves about unimportant details, and relate events obscured and colored by what they wish had happened instead of what actually did happen.

I've never forgotten the story the way he told it to me that day, and he didn't really tell me all of it, because a man only sees something like that from one viewpoint. Uncle Tom told me some of it, because he knew Toby Wheeler. Uncle Aschom told me some of it because he knew Harry Bailey. Anna Maria Shorter told me some of it, because she knew Ed Shorter like no one else on this earth. And some of it I just know. I don't know how I know it, or where I heard it, but I just know that this was the way it happened.

CHAPTER

3

"The weather is a fool."
My Uncle Aschom often says this.

HE LIT a cigar, puffed it contentedly for a moment, rocking back and forth in the chair. "I remember the winter of 1904," he said. And as he spoke, suddenly it was all there. I could see every bit of it, spread out before me. The raw edge of late afternoon that had sent people hurrying for the warmth of their firesides. Darkness settling over the city. When he spoke of it I could see the people gathered before their open fires, I could picture the rich, warm red furnishings in the room, the walnut paneling, and the sparkle of Stieff silver.

I could see the harbor. The *Shanghai Greyhound,* a rust bucket, Uncle John called her, inbound from the Philippines with a load of Manila hemp, nudging slowly up the channel, dropping her hook in the fairway instead of docking. The gas lights flickering at the street corners. The muffled sound of horses' hoofs on the cobblestone streets, white with snow. The sound of sleigh bells on the rig coming down Light

54

Street. The tall schooners and rams and pungys and bugeyes tied along the waterfront, snow drifting down quietly through their rigging. And just a few feet up, out of the lee of the buildings, a half a gale roared in out of the northeast. Nothing was moving on the Bay, and nothing, except for a small amount of inbound ocean commerce, had moved for three and a half weeks, as one blizzard after another hurled itself across the Eastern Shore and battered at the crippled city.

"And we didn't see the sun at all. Not for three and a half weeks we didn't see it. Every time the snow would stop the wind would blow even harder, and it would get colder and nasty and raw and the clouds would lift a little and there would be a lot of scud under them and you could see a little bit farther, but the wind blew and the sun never came out. I never saw anything like it either before or since."

It wasn't just that it snowed. It often did that in the winter time in Baltimore. But these snow storms were of a pattern that had never been seen before. The normal snow storm lasted anywhere from a few hours to a full day at the most, and then the weather cleared. In the normal winter there were six, seven, and sometimes a few more of these short storms. But usually, after each one, and certainly after two, a person could expect the weather to clear. And when it did the sun would come out, the snow would melt, and the ground was usually bare and soggy before the next snow fall. But this time the storms came like the regular, inexorable beat of a strong heart. The old-timers shook their heads and wondered, the children played and frolicked, building snow forts and snow men of remarkable endurance, and the ships stayed in port. The docks were filled with goods for shipment and certain items were in very short supply.

Uncle John was forty-two years old that winter. He was a successful, seasoned captain, financially solvent and secure, with the full ownership of a fine, 90-foot schooner, a solid, substantial home in the city, completely paid for, and a comfortable savings account in the Baltimore Trust Company. But it had been three and a half weeks since he had made port with a cargo, and the Christmas season was just a week away from being a reality. The store windows were already decorated, there were whispered conversations and giggles, and wives talked of baking cookies. John Talbott had two young sons and a small daughter who had come to expect generous visits from Santa Claus, and now he was faced with the prospect of dipping into the carefully assembled savings account rather than spending current income to make the old gentleman's visit one they would never forget.

With a certain sadness, he knew that this would probably be the last Christmas there would be a Santa Claus for the two boys. He was certain that Jack was believing this year only because he desperately wanted to believe, thus retaining some of the magic for himself. He knew full well the signs, the small slips, the wavering of the belief, the slightly embarrassed look that came to his face sometimes when he spoke of Santa Claus. And he knew that next year there would be no aura of Christmas for his oldest boy; his eyes would be fully opened. And the youngest, Richard, would certainly know too. It just worked that way. Then there would only be little Ellen to still believe and keep the magic of Christmas in the Talbott house for a few more years.

He was a successful businessman, but he was, in his own mind, a man badly in need of a payday, and he knew that down in the Patuxent there were oyster houses stocked with all of the oysters his boat could hold. And he was sure that down there someplace, most anyplace, he imagined, there was a market for the load of coal that had been put aboard the *Albatross* two weeks earlier. And he knew that the price would be high at both ends of the trip because of the lack of movement in the past three and a half weeks. As a matter of fact, he knew that if he was the first captain to make port with a load of fresh oysters for the holiday season he could just about name his own price.

As he swung down the gangplank and plodded across the snow-covered street he glanced back at the *Shanghai Greyhound,* her riding light a barely visible glow through the snow. He recalled her tired and beaten look as her skipper paid out her anchor chain and she swung slowly around in the current. Her decks, bridge, and spars had been covered with snow, and still were, and it hadn't let up, not even a little bit, in the last four hours. He knew that out the other side of North Point the Bay was a dusty, heaving, pitching, raw green hell. He wished he could have a few words with the skipper of the *Shanghai Greyhound,* wished he could talk with him about the weather he had left behind down the Bay, perhaps get some inkling of whether or not it had been any better where he had come from.

Uncle John rubbed his chin with the back of his hand and tried to remember the last Bay boat that had made port. It seemed a long time ago, and the more he thought about it the more certain he was that nothing had come in since the *Westmoreland* nosed her way up the harbor just after the snow settled in for good and proper. He had talked to her captain the night after she came in, talked with him in the tavern across the street from where he was standing right now, and the captain had told him about the rugged trip up the Bay from the mouth of the Potomac. They were standing

57

at the bar together, cutting the chill of the storm with a mug of hot buttered rum.

"It was a rough trip all the way up, John. Kept getting worse all the time. It started snowing just as we cast off at Solomons, and by the time we had cleared Drum Point it was a blizzard. The wind was east-north-east and blowing hard. Once we got out into the Bay it was blowing too hard and it was too rough to go at standard speed so I rang her down. When we turned to go up, almost broadside to the wind— thank you, John, I will have one—she was rolling so bad she was rolling her paddles all the way out of the water. We never did see Cove Point when we went by. You couldn't see more than a quarter of a mile out there."

He paused and lit the cigar. "I was in the wheelhouse with the quartermaster and mate when all of a sudden I looked out the window on the starboard side and there was this barque off there about a hundred yards, just abaft abeam, couldn't have been more than a hundred yards away. She just loomed up out of the snow all of a sudden like. I looked and there she was, no warning at all. She was smashing her way up the Bay to beat all hell, carrying canvas to beat the band. She was carrying a jib and her foretopmast staysail, all of her main and mizzen staysails, a spanker, and fore, main, and mizzen topsails, upper and lower."

"The hell she was!"

"So help me God she was! She was loaded too. My, this is a good cigar, John. Thank you again. Low in the water, heeled over, just plowing into that seaway like it wasn't even there. She wasn't rolling or hobby-horsing. Just smashing right through it, throwing it all over the place. I don't know what kind of a load she was carrying, but she was loaded deep and she certainly was steady. And moving. My God, she was moving!

"I pointed her out to the quartermaster and told him to steer clear of her, and we came off to port a little. If we hadn't I guess we might have run her down. I opened the door and went out on the bridge to watch her. Hell, a man don't see a sight like that every day anymore."

"He certainly doesn't."

"And you know something, John. She was overhauling us, not us overhauling her. Of course we were only moving half speed, but he was carrying sail and she was moving. God, she was moving."

"Those old bastards aren't afraid of a damn thing, are they?"

"If you'd been around the Horn a couple of times you wouldn't be either. Anyways, just as I came out on the bridge and looked over at her, I heard this voice. John, it was the deepest voice I ever heard in my life. Sounded like a nineteen-foot bullfrog with a helluva cold. I heard it plain as anything. 'AHOY THERE, CAP'N, CAN YOU GIVE US A SHEER!' "

"He's used to being out there all by himself."

"Yes, I suppose he is. Well, we stood off from him and paralleled his course for a while, but pretty soon that barque was gone out of sight ahead of us, just tearing up the Bay. When we got in to the harbor she was already unloaded, sitting out there in the fairway half out of the water."

He remembered the conversation clearly, and looked around, out across the harbor, to see if she was still there. And she was, still swinging at her mooring just off shore, but she was low in the water again. She was loaded again, waiting like all the rest of them for a break in the weather so she could go down the Bay.

He continued plodding through the snow toward the tavern across the street. Its windows were warm and inviting

59

through the snow. As he reached the middle of the street he stopped and looked up into the teeth of the gale. When he had gone back aboard the *Albatross* after dinner the wind had been straight out of the northeast, but now, as he thoughtfully turned his head from side to side, his sensitive ear lobes detected a decided shift to the north. "North-northeast," he muttered. "But still blowing half a gale." He studied this bit of information, turning it over slowly in his mind, examining it and trying to fit it into the pattern of things.

Standing there on the snow-covered street, John Talbott would have presented somewhat of a problem to the inland city dweller seeking to describe him, but the residents of the Bay country would have had no trouble. They would have simply described him as a waterman and felt that this was adequate. He had the face of a man somewhat older than his forty-two years. It had a leathery, deeply lined look about it, but it was a face that smiled easily, and his eyes were the clearest blue imaginable. All in all however, smile or no, it was a face that could best be described as determined, and even the casual observer would have known that this was the face of a man secure in the knowledge that he was competent to stand up against anything that might be thrown against him.

The rest of his body, however, was not at all like that of an older man, or even that of the usual man his age. Beneath the warm clothing he was wearing was the body of a young athlete in top physical condition. He was six feet tall, powerfully built, with heavily muscled arms and legs that had been developed by years aloft in the rigging or straining at the end of a hawser or halyard. And he carried himself with an air of dignity and determination that radiated to all those around him, and made men willing to follow him anywhere.

After studying the wind for several minutes he turned in his tracks and walked back toward the *Albatross*. He went aboard. He went down the ladder to his cabin. He lit the oil lamp and studied the barometer. He reached up and tapped the glass face with his index finger. The needle, which had been resting at 29.36, took a slight jump and settled at 29.38. The glass was rising. He turned to his desk, opened the logbook, and traced the history of the barometer settings for the past three and a half weeks.

He went to the deep shelf that ran the fore and aft length of his cabin, serving as a chart table and plotting board, took a piece of paper and his parallel rules, and made a graph of the settings shown in the logbook. He stood up and looked down at it, trying to find what it was that seemed to be the key to something he knew he was working toward. Without taking his eyes off the graph he reached into a drawer under the shelf and took out a cigar. He lit it, still studying the graph. He stood there for a long time. The cabin filled with smoke. His eyes began to water and he wiped them with the tips of his fingers. He tried to get the beginnings of the train of thought he was seeking, but it continued to elude him.

Between each low point plotted on the graph, each representing a period of snowfall, the line went up and then came back down again. But was it a period of snowfall? He assumed it was, but he wasn't positive. He went back to the logbook and went back over the time, noting the weather at each low point. He was right. It was snowing, and snowing hard, at each of the low points. But that wasn't it. That wasn't what he was looking for. He had been sure of that before he started the graph. After each period of snowfall the line came

61

up again. He had been sure of that too.

But here was something, and this was significant! Each time it went deeper, each time it snowed, and it never quite rose to what it had been before. But there was something else. What was that thing that was nagging at him? What was the key to this? He went back to the log, and plotted in the wind direction for each barometer setting. That was it! The wind had never gone beyond northeast. It had only gone that far the last time, as a matter of fact, and then it had backed around again, east, southeast, and then south. But the last time it had gone to northeast, and this time it had gone past it. "Many a time," he thought, "I've seen the glass drop and drop, watched the wind go around from east to northeast, north-north-east, then north, and then boom in out of the northwest, the glass start to rise, and the top blow off."

He went over and tapped the barometer again. It ticked a little, not a full tenth, but a little. "I wish we knew more about the weather," he thought.

He left the cabin, realizing once he got out into the fresh air how smoky and close it had been down there. He stopped again at the foot of the gangplank and felt the wind on his ear lobes. He heard the clock on the board strike once and then heard the booming bell in a steeple not far away. Eight-thirty. He turned and studied the *Albatross*. He looked the length of her, then turned his eyes aloft into the rigging. He went back on board, struck a match and looked at the thermometer hanging on the after bulkhead on her main cabin trunk. Thirty-four degrees. It was sheltered from the wind, though, and early in the evening, and he knew it was colder out on the Bay, and would get colder as the night progressed.

"I wonder if I'm right," he thought. "This could certainly be the last one. If I could get out of here tonight, with the ebb tide, it will be the top of the flood season soon, if I can do that—if I will do it—I'll have a following wind and an ebb tide all the way down to Solomons." He turned that thought over in his mind. "Suppose I run down and it doesn't clear off, suppose I miss the mouth of the Patuxent, suppose I don't see Cove Point Light? What do I do then?"

If he left at the top of the flood tide, got out in good order, if it continued to blow like it was blowing, he would pass Cove Point in the darkness. He would have to see that light. He wouldn't run the risk of turning purely on the basis of elapsed time and estimated speed on a night like this. Too much could happen too fast if he was wrong. He didn't care if Raney Tongue did do it all the time. He didn't do it on a night like this. If he didn't see that light, what would he do?

His feet were getting cold but his eyes were clear and the wind had swept out his mind. He could always warm his feet in the tavern, but the cold had brought a clarity to his mind and he wanted to retain it for a few minutes more while he thought this thing out. He stomped his feet several times, which knocked the snow off his boots but accomplished little more.

Would he go if it was not snowing? If it was just a half a gale out of the northeast, temperature say about forty or forty-five? He nodded. He knew he would, given the same economic conditions. Would he do it if it was just a snow storm? Wind about ten to fifteen knots, maybe even twenty? He nodded again. Of course he would. He had done that before too. He puffed on the cigar, bit off a ragged end, and spit it into the snow.

What was holding him back? Why was he so hesitant? No! Let's turn that around. What was making him so all-fired eager to go? What was giving him the itch to get moving? Nothing had really changed. Nothing he could definitely point to. It was still snowing hard. The wind was still blowing somewhere between thirty and forty knots. Nothing had really changed. Nothing except what he had found by making that graph. And even considering that, nothing had changed. Nothing except his own attitude. He had seen something on that graph that offered a reasonable chance that this might be the last snow storm in the seemingly endless parade. Had he really seen it? Was it just a hunch? He shook his head. No, he didn't think it was just a hunch. He knew he couldn't make a case for it with many people, but it was more than a hunch.

It was a well-reasoned judgment, based on what he thought was sound information, interpreted with experience gained over the years. It wasn't a hunch. "Which sounds very grand and wise," he thought. "But I want to go. I want to make this trip. I need the money. But do I need it badly enough to risk my boat and my crew on something I'm not really certain about? What if I don't see Cove Point Light? If it's still snowing this hard I certainly won't see it unless I run aground. If the time runs out and I don't see it what will I do then?"

Again he turned the picture over, exposing the reason he had picked Solomons Island in the first place. "That's obvious," he thought. "It's the closest place where I know I can unload my coal and take on oysters. Cambridge is no good. They have the railroad and they'll have coal. But if I can't see Cove Point Light, well, I'll just keep going. To the Potomac. To Kinsale or Smith's Creek. It'll be daylight by then and I can edge in toward shore. If I keep using the lead line, keep track of the bottom, maybe I can find where I am on the chart if I don't see anything. And I'll know when I'm off

64

the mouth of the Potomac, I'm not worried about that. But Solomons is the place. The only way those people could get coal would be for us to bring it, and they must be beginning to get cold about now and that's home. I wish it was a little warmer, though." He looked back up into the rigging of the *Albatross*. "We'll have to worry about ice all night long."

He stomped his feet again. "Christ, it's cold out here."

Toby Wheeler walked through the snow. It was wet and sloshed around his sea boots. He turned at the corner and saw two men waiting in the doorway. He came up alongside them and without a word the three of them turned into the entrance of a small tavern. It was warm in the room and a fire crackled on the hearth. Toby liked this place. A man could get a good meal here, one that filled him, without paying too much for it. They went to a table and ordered dinner. "I sure wish we could get some oysters," Toby said, not to anyone in particular.

"We have oysters," the woman said.

"You have!"

She nodded and smiled smugly.

"I didn't think there were any oysters left in Baltimore," Toby said.

"Depends on where you look for them, Mr. Wheeler," the woman said with a tolerant smile. "We've had a few of them all along. Not too many, but enough for our friends. And we've still got some."

The men each ordered and ate a dozen oysters on the half shell before they filled themselves with the steaming, hearty beef stew that was the specialty of the tavern. Toby ate the oysters, although he was worried as he ate them. They didn't taste exactly right to him, but he watched the others as they ate, and if they tasted the slight off-color flavor they certainly didn't act as if they did. "I'm getting right tired of this sittin' on my ass in port." Toby looked up from his stew and smiled at Edward Shorter, who had just spoken.

"Rather be out there tonight freezing your ass instead of sitting on it here where it's warm?"

Ed Shorter looked at him and smiled. It was a gentle smile for such a hard-looking man. He had a leathery face, deeply tanned in spite of the month of the year, friendly brown eyes, and that easy grace of a big man who knows he has nothing to fear or prove. "I think I would, Toby. Two weeks ago I wouldn't've." The others were watching him. "I reckon if Cap'n John said to go it would be all right with me. I'd welcome it, for a fact I would. It ain't so bad out there tonight that I ain't seen it a helluva lot worse."

Toby leaned forward, resting his huge forearms on the table. He looked at Harry Bailey and grinned. "Any minute now he's gonna tell you it isn't near as bad as doubling the Horn. Isn't that right, Bull? Nothing like going around the old Horn, is there? Just a little mill pond out there." He snorted. "I like it fine right here where I am. If Cap'n John happened to say, 'Let's take a little trip down the Bay tonight,' well, I reckon I'd go along with him all right, but I for one hope to hell he doesn't get any wild ideas like going down the Bay in a roarin' blizzard. Now what the hell's all this talk about taking a trip down the Bay in a blizzard anyway? Who says we're apt to be doing anything as silly as that?"

"Nobody said anything about going down the Bay, Toby. I just said a man gets tired of sitting around port where his wife can bother him. A little bit at a time is all right, but I ain't used to it in such large doses for such a long period of time, that's all."

Toby leaned back in his chair. "I doubt if we're gonna be doing anything like that tonight." He looked at Ed Shorter and grinned. "Sorry, Bull. Maybe the weather will break tomorrow and you can get away from your old lady for a couple of days."

On a low bluff overlooking the mouth of the Patuxent River, on the east side of Solomons Island, in the parlor of a large, two-story, crab-fat yellow, clapboard house, Robert Cook stood at the window, contemplating the snow falling in his front yard. He could not see the river, although it was less than one hundred feet away. He could not even see the other side of the road that ran in front of his house, between his front yard and where the ground dropped off to the shore.

All he could see was the swirling snow as it drifted in under the roof of the front porch and settled on the canvas tarpaulin that covered a cord of firewood stacked close to the front door. He could tell by the drift of the snow and the sound of the wind that the most important factor of the storm had remained unchanged in the last hour. The wind was still out of the northeast.

He walked back to the large, pot-bellied stove, turned his back to it, and stood looking out into the room, warming his back. He was thinking about his supplies of coal, and the more he thought about it the more concerned he became, not only with the idea of running out of something people would pay for with their good money, but worried about what would happen to those people when there was no more coal to sell to them. In all the years he had run his feed and coal business his supplies had never been as low as they were now.

Since he was not in the grocery business he was not closely concerned with the supplies of food on hand in the surrounding countryside, but he had thought about this matter and it gave him no great cause for alarm. With the exception of the people on the island itself, most of whom were merchants and watermen, the people along the shoreline of the Patuxent, and back in the creeks, were farmers who raised a large amount of their own food. He knew they could be counted on to have canned and preserved ample supplies of staple food to take them through the winter. The extra items that came home with them from trips to town on Saturday were things they could do without for the time being if necessary.

But there was one other thing he was concerned about, and it was also an item he carried in stock in his warehouse. It was coal oil. He was running very low on coal oil, and he was certain there were some people living up the river who must be completely out by now, since he had not been able to send his pungy up the river in over three weeks. The pungy was thirty-eight feet long. She was his delivery wagon, the way he kept his customers supplied. In normal times she made two trips a week up the river as far as Benedict, stopping at the wharfs along the way to drop off drums of coal oil and consignments of coal.

The coal oil was used in the lamps that lit most of the homes in the area, and without it many of his friends and customers would be reduced to lighting with candles, if they had any. In addition, some people had small, coal oil stoves, used to heat bedrooms usually, and he supposed there would be many people going to bed tonight in cold bedrooms. But the coal was the main thing that was concerning him, far more than coal oil, because almost everybody heated the major portions of their homes with coal stoves. "If this

68

weather doesn't break soon," he thought, "a lot of people are going to be in trouble. This thing sure does make a man feel isolated and alone. Most of the time, with the steamers and sailboats coming and going regularly, it isn't that way. But it takes something like this to make a man realize how dependent we are on the boats."

Across the mouth of the harbor, directly opposite the steamer wharf, projecting out over the water on pilings, was the oyster house. There was no sign on it saying "Oyster House"; this was not the name of a business, and it was never referred to as Wood's Oyster House. Just the oyster house.

It was sheltered from the northeast wind by the high ground and tall trees behind it, but even with this protection the wind moaned around it, leaked through its loose-fitting wooden walls, and rattled its haphazardly applied shingles. The entire structure sagged slightly on the southeast corner, and the whitewash that had been freshly applied to the outside in the fall was almost completely weathered away.

No one lived in the oyster house, and no one was there on this cold night. There was really no reason for anyone to be there. No one would come seeking to buy oysters on a night like this. The owner of the oyster house, Henry Wood, was home before his fire, content in the knowledge that when the weather did break, and the boats came down the Bay from Baltimore, he had a house full of oysters, tonged with great physical discomfort between the series of snowstorms that had hit the island.

He was not altogether happy about the price he might get for them, since most of the oyster houses in the river were also full, and he knew that the first boat that arrived would see the oyster beds covered with boats tonging for more oysters.

69

All a captain had to do was anchor somewhere nearby and buy directly. But he also knew that the first boat down would be in a hurry to get loaded and be the first boat back to Baltimore, and there was something to be said for the fact that he had better than a boatload of oysters already on hand, and that he had a crew of men to load that boat quickly and get her on her way. He was sure that other houses could offer the same, but his house happened to be the closest to the mouth of the river, and thus the closest to Baltimore. He knew this would be a talking point when he discussed the price of his oysters. He wished he had more of an advantage than this, but it was better than nothing.

He hoped the first boat down would bring a load of coal. He was getting very low on coal and he knew that Cook's warehouse was dangerously low, considering the number of people they supplied.

Uncle John walked toward the tavern. He wished he could make up his mind. The factors seemed almost perfectly balanced, and he was unable to find a single thing that could tip the scales one way or the other. If the wind would shift a little more before the top of the tide—well, he'd see about that.

CHAPTER

4

"He was gambling because he had to, but the cards he held were good cards and he was a skillful player."

From *Fate is the Hunter,* by Ernest K. Gann.

"I COULDN'T make up my mind what to do, son. I knew I wanted to go. But it was an awful night, and I knew I'd be running a risk, and I didn't know if it made sense to try it. I knew that once I got out on the Bay there was no turning back, too. Oh, I knew that all right. I kept hoping the wind would shift, the snow would stop, something would happen to make up my mind for me. I reckon I was looking for some sort of omen or somebody to say I should go. But there wasn't anybody that could tell me that. Being captain of a big schooner's a lonely thing sometimes."

He pulled open the door and walked into the warmth of the tavern. The room roared with the activity of a full house. Its tables were crowded with sailors held in port by the weather, the bar was elbow to elbow with laughing, shouting men, and their pent-up energy was evident in every exaggerated gesture and every shouted word. He nodded to several men he knew, looked around for some of his crew but didn't see them, wondered briefly where they might be, then made his way to the large, round table in the front corner, which by unspoken agreement was the Captains' Table. Three men looked up as he approached and nodded their greetings. Each was fortifying himself with a steaming tankard of hot buttered rum. He signaled the barkeep and sat down.

Captain Tom Webster, sixty-four last October, a huge man with a great white beard, owner of the *Hattie Travers*, was regaling them with an account of his last trip to the Rappahannock. He had made port during the first of the series of blizzards. "You couldn't see a hundred feet in any direction, wind blowin' like a fool, the mate frettin' and stewin' and sayin' we'd missed the damn buoy. So I heaved the lead, got me a pretty tasty little mess of mud, and told him to ease her off a point. As luck would have it, 'bout three minutes later we damn near ran the thing down. You know there ain't no mud in the Bay that tastes like that stuff just before you get to that spar. Sure as hell it don't taste like that stuff inshore from it—John, what in the hell is on your mind? You look like you ain't even with us."

Uncle John was not paying much attention to the story. He was still thinking about whether or not he should make a try at the Bay and he looked up from his mug of hot buttered rum with a startled look. He forgot for a moment where he was and spoke before he considered what he was saying. "I think we're due for a break in the weather tonight, and I'm trying to make up my mind whether or not to get my boys together and go down the Bay tonight."

"Tonight!"

Uncle John nodded. "Sounds crazy, doesn't it?"

72

Harry Marshall, who had leaned forward with interest mixed with disbelief at the first mention of a change in the weather, grunted. "Sounds kinda unusual, I'm forced to admit, but it don't sound crazy, not comin' from you it don't. What the hell makes you think we're due for a change in the weather?"

"Don't look like it's changed none to me," Tom Webster said, turning in his chair and looking out the window.

"Didn't say it had. Just said I thought it might." He had become hesitant when he noticed the interest of Harry Marshall. He saw that Billy Duke was watching him too. He was suddenly sorry he had said anything at all about going down the Bay.

"Well," Billy Duke said, "what makes you think it might, John?"

He shrugged. "I don't know. This has been going on for so damn long. It's got to stop some time."

"That's for certain," Harry Marshall said. "The world's comin' to an end someday too. There's preachers up in town who say it's gonna be tomorrow. Every day they say it's gonna be tomorrow. But it ain't ended yet. And every couple of days I hear somebody say it's gonna stop snowing tomorrow. I reckon as long as this wind keeps blowin' in from out of the northeast it could keep on snowin' forever if the wind blew forever. And why the hell couldn't it, when you get right down to it? Three days ago I said this was the last one. But here it is snowin' again today. That ain't really the reason you think the weather's gonna break, is it?"

Uncle John looked down at the table top. "I've just got a feeling, that's all."

"Now I'd take that for an answer from Tom here," Billy said. "But not from you, John. You've got more than that to back it up."

Uncle John took another sip of rum, giving himself time to think about his answer. "I've got to get off this subject," he thought. "I want to go, and I might, but if I do I don't want half the harbor leaving with me."

He looked down at the table again, then looked up with a self-conscious grin, the best he could manage. He wished he could even blush a little. "Well," he said sheepishly, "well—I was reading in the—the—*Hagerstown Almanac* today—"

Tom Webster exploded with laughter. Heads turned as he threw back his head and roared but he paid no attention, continuing to laugh until he almost choked. The laughter ended in a fit of coughing, and finally, wiping the tears from his eyes, he blew his nose and said, "Well, by God! I've heard everything now. John Talbott reading the *Hagerstown Almanac*—and believing it."

"I didn't say I believed it. You don't see me casting off and going down the channel, do you? I was just thinking—suppose they're right?"

Billy Duke drained his cup and pushed back his chair. He looked at Harry Marshall. "It's a sad day, a sad day indeed, when John Talbott, John Talbott of all people, consorts with the *Hagerstown Almanac*." He stood up. "What's your horoscope for today, John? Something like 'Today is a good day for traveling'? The trouble with you, John, is that you're getting tired of having the *Albatross* laying over there at the wharf with a cargo on her and no place to go with it."

He took his hat down from the hook on the wall. "Well, you men can sit here and discuss all of this supernatural tommyrot if you want to, but me, I'm going home to my good wife and fireside, and tomorrow morning, if I can find my way through the blizzard, I'll come down and say good morning to you."

Harry Marshall pushed back his chair and got up to leave. "I'll go with you, Billy." He looked down at the two men remaining at the table. "Tell him you feel lucky, John. Tell him you found a four-leaf clover or something. All you need is a little luck and Tom'll go with you. He believes in luck, you know that. And damn if I don't think that's better than the *Hagerstown Almanac* when you come right down to it."

Suddenly he slipped into the chair next to Uncle John. "Don't do it, John," he said, his voice filled with mock emotion. "Oh, please don't do it, John. Think of your poor wife and children on this stormy night. Go home to them, John. After all—" he started to snicker—"if anything happens they can't sue the *Hagerstown Almanac*."

All three men were laughing now, and Uncle John joined them. Finally he held up his hands and said, "A man's got to believe in something, and it seemed as good as anything after the weather we've been having."

"Well, it'll break sometime, John. Let's hope to hell it's soon," Billy Duke said as the two men turned away from the table. "We'll see you tomorrow," he added, and it seemed to Uncle John that he said it in a normal manner, as though he really meant it.

He and Tom Webster watched the two men leave the tavern.

"What do you think?" Tom Webster asked.

"What do you mean?" Uncle John replied.

"I mean do you think they believed you? All that stuff? You know damn well what I mean."

"Believed what?"

"That hogwash about it all being a joke and you got the idea out of the *Almanac*. Because even if they did, I didn't.

75

Now what's on your mind, by God? I know there's something, but I don't aim to have it too crowded out there tonight either."

Uncle John looked at him steadily, but said nothing.

"Look John, they may have believed you—"

The same steady gaze, then the beginnings of a smile. "Do you think they did?"

"I don't know. We'll walk out in a little while and take a look at their boats, see what they're doing, if anything. I hope they did, though."

"I wish I hadn't been so free to speak."

"I wish I hadn't asked you what was on your mind."

"Well, I said it before I thought about it. I wasn't going to tell anybody."

"Do you really think the weather's gonna break?"

"I don't know. And I don't know if I'm going down the Bay tonight either, in spite of all this talk. If it doesn't break I'd be in a helluva spot. I've been thinking about it, but so far I haven't made up my mind. I just don't know about this weather. But I've been studying it, and I really think it's going to break and clear off, maybe by morning."

"And what makes you think anything like that?"

He knew it was a very long string of pure theory, but nevertheless he told him about the graph, about the way the barometer had behaved, and told him about the wind.

"Where was the wind when you came in, John?"

"North-north-east, and still blowing half a gale. But I'll bet by this time tomorrow it'll be straight out of the northwest."

Tom Webster's eyes lit up. "That's a shift, all right. I've seen it do that before and clear up, but I've also seen it do it and not clear up. I don't know. With a little luck— What are you carrying, John, coal?"

76

"Yep. Full load. Been aboard for three weeks, just waiting to go."

"Well, by God, if you get it there, and with a little luck I don't doubt that you will, you'll surely get a smart price for it. Hell of a lot more than you'll have to pay for those oysters you're gonna bring back and make a killing on, I'll wager. There may be an 'R' in December, but you'd never know it with what the weather's done to the oyster market. I'll wager there ain't a fresh oyster in Baltimore, and with the holidays comin' on who can tell what that first boatload of fresh ones will bring. You might even get your name in the papers besides." He smiled, waved his arm expansively, and said, "Hell, John, you'd probably be the man of the hour."

It was pretty obvious what was coming and Uncle John looked at the old man knowingly and smiled. "Look at him," he said. "Just like an old firehorse when the bell rings. Thinkin' of trying it yourself, Cap'n Tom? Got an idea of being the man of the hour yourself? Maybe you'd like to see your name in the paper? How 'bout it? Is the old master going to favor us with his presence on the Bay tonight?"

"Yes, by God, I am thinking about it. And I'm not too old to have a go at it in spite of the weather, in case you're thinkin' that might be the case. You might get the top price for those oysters, but I feel lucky, and by damn I might just go along to make sure you earn it. If you don't mind I think you might have a real race on your hands. You wouldn't mind a little company out there, would you, John?"

"I don't reckon I've got much choice, do I? No, I don't mind a little company, Cap'n Tom, but I certainly hope Billy and Harry don't get any wild ideas."

"Well, if we don't show a lot of activity for a little while I figure they'll think you were joking. You're loaded, so all you

77

have to do is get your crew together. How long do you think that will take?"

"Tide turns at 10:42. We'll be ready by then. Are you loaded too, Cap'n Tom, or are you just going after the oysters?"

"Oh, I'm loaded. No one-way trips for me. But don't let it bother you. I'm carrying coal oil so I don't reckon it'll hurt the price of your coal none if I go along. As a matter of fact, I reckon they'll be damn glad to see both of us. But I'm loaded, so all I have to do is get my crew and go. I'm glad of that, because we don't want a lot of pulling and hauling over there until the last minute."

"Then you really think it makes sense to go? You act like there's nothing much to it."

"Well, I wouldn't say that. But I do think it makes sense to take a good look at the weather in a couple of minutes, and then decide. But I've had a feeling in my bones all day long that the time was comin' when this storm would break. And now you come along and tell me why I had this feeling. I'm inclined to feel that it probably will be all right to go, unless of course you like the warmth of your bed too much to leave, but I think we ought to watch the weather right up to the last minute, without being too damn obvious about it, of course."

"Suppose we don't see Cove Point Light?"

"Well, it'll be dark then, and if it's still snowing and we don't see it, I think we ought to keep right on going. Sail until morning, then move in close to the shore until we get to the mouth of the Potomac."

That was what Uncle John wanted to hear. He put his hands on the table, palms down. "Exactly what I thought! Exactly! We're agreed?" He lowered his voice. "Depending

78

on how the weather looks, we'll sail at the top of the tide?"

"Hell yes, we're agreed. We will sail at the top of the tide. Let's walk out of here and take a look at the weather now and see what's doing."

They stepped out into the street. The gale still roared overhead, but in the lee of the building they could only hear it, only knew it was there by the sound, not the feel. They walked across the wide street, gradually feeling the wind pressure increasing against their backs. Without any sign of communication, when they reached a certain spot in the street, unmarked and no different from any other spot, they turned in unison and lifted their faces to the wind.

Tom Webster was the first to speak. "You're right, John. It has shifted, and with a little luck it should blow this stuff out of here by tomorrow. I think we should go. I feel lucky, and it's nice to know you've given me a logical reason to feel that way. Now look, John, it's gonna be a mite knobby out there tonight, I don't need to tell you that. So I think it would be a very good idea if we kept each other company on the way down. If you agree, and want to do likewise, we'll hang lanterns in our yawl davits so we can keep each other in sight. If we do that there won't be much chance of us runnin' together. But by God, you'll have to find your own way back because I'm not going to sit around down there waiting for you."

They walked back toward the building to get out of the wind. They stood there several minutes, two figures in the snow, silhouetted against the windows of the tavern, then turned and moved apart. "And John," Tom Webster said as Uncle John turned away, "a ten dollar gold piece says I get top price for the oysters."

"Done," Uncle John said softly over his shoulder. He

walked back across the street toward the slip where the *Albatross* was moored. He remembered that he hadn't seen any of his crew in the tavern and thought he would take one more look at the barometer before he went looking for them in the tavern where he knew he would find them.

Toby Wheeler looked at the fire roaring on the hearth of the tavern. It was hot and stuffy in the room and he felt very uncomfortable. He wished he hadn't eaten so much beef stew. He also wished he hadn't eaten those oysters. He could feel the sweat on his forehead. His stomach felt slightly unsettled. He took a final swallow of coffee, pushed back his chair, and stood up. "I think we might as well get out of here and get some fresh air. It's hot as hell in this damn place."

The others joined him as they paid their bill and filed out through the doorway into the cold. The fresh air felt good as it struck his face. His stomach began to settle down as he walked down the street breathing deeply. The perspiration on his face felt very cold and he wiped the sleeve of his coat across his forehead. He was still concerned about the taste of the oysters, and he wondered if that had anything to do with the way he had felt in the tavern. As they passed under a street lamp he searched the faces of the other men. They seemed to be walking along without any trouble, and there was certainly nothing on their faces to indicate that they were experiencing any unusual feelings.

The men reached the corner, and then, for no good reason that any one one of them could have stated, they all turned toward the waterfront. They had walked only a few steps in that direction, the wind now at their backs, when they all suddenly became aware of the direction they had taken. They began to look at each other. They all seemed to be waiting for someone to remind them they had taken the wrong turn. Finally Ed Shorter grunted. "Well, we might as well walk on down there and see what the hell's going on. Nothing wrong with that, is there? We can—well, we can see Harry safely home. Make sure he don't get lost along the way."

Harry Bailey looked at him and laughed. "Just don't want to go home, do you, Bull?"

After that, no one spoke, and they kept walking.

Harry Bailey felt the thrill of companionship go through him as they walked through the snow. These were men! Real men! No panty-waists here. He was conscious that his walk had become almost a swagger. He just couldn't seem to help it. They had accepted him and he was one of them, and they were walking through the snow toward the waterfront where there were other men, real men, and anything might happen. They might get into a real brawl and he could stand beside them and fight. They might go down the Bay tonight. They might. He almost wished they would. Three and a half weeks was too long for a man to be in port, and this blizzard was nothing that these men couldn't handle, and he could help them. After three trips they were beginning to trust him, and he knew that meant a great deal. On the last trip they had told him what to do and taken it for granted that he would do it. There had been no helping him, or showing him, or telling him, then watching to make certain he did it right.

He looked back over his shoulder to see if anyone was following them. The street was clear. There was no one. He gave a sigh of relief. There had been a man in the tavern, a well-dressed man, sitting alone, who had spent a great deal of time looking at him. He could have been a Pinkerton man. Harry Bailey knew that his father would spare no expense and go to any effort to find his son and drag him back into the banking business. It was a long way from Indianapolis, but his father had the money and he was determined that his son should come into the bank, without ever asking Harry what he thought of the idea.

He had selected the schools that Harry attended and insisted that Harry work in the bank during the summer vacations so he could learn the fundamentals. For three summers Harry saw those fundamentals in operation and he hated every minute of it. He realized that you looked down your nose at anyone who really needed what you had to offer. You treated them as though they somehow did not belong to the human race. You managed their small amounts of money, being careful to give them the impression you were doing them a favor, and you got wealthy off what you did with the large amount of money that those little individual accounts represented. But you treated those people as something to be barely tolerated.

He had worked in a cage as a teller (learn it all, his father said), and he had watched these people come into the bank with an air of not being at all comfortable. They seemed to change as they came through the door. He met some of them occasionally on the outside and found them decent, law-abiding, normal citizens who loved life and walked in fear of no man, or so it seemed. But he had seen them come into the bank, slightly stooped, apprehensive, and looking out of the corners of their eyes from side to side. They spoke softly and said "sir," even to him.

And then there were the others, the ones who didn't really need what you had to offer. There were other banks that would welcome them, and they knew it. They were to be flattered and fawned over, and you were told to take whatever abuse they might care to hand out. You looked down your nose at the others, but you looked straight up the ass of these people. He would never have thought of that particular phrase in Indianapolis. It came to him one afternoon in late September as he stood his trick at the wheel. The wind was gentle and he had time to contemplate his situation.

It all came to a head on a day in August. He walked to the doorway of his father's office—there was a question about cashing a large check—and stopped, seeing that his father was occupied. The man, whom he saw only from the back, was standing before his father's desk—leaning across it was closer to the truth—shaking his finger and saying in soft but acrid tones, "Now you listen to me, you son-of-a-bitch, I want this done. I don't give a damn what you say. I want it done, do you hear! And if it isn't done, I'll pull all of my business accounts out of this bank, and I can see to it that at least fifty more come out of here as well, and the walls of this hallowed establishment will come tumbling down like the walls of Jericho. Now you do what I say, God damn it! Do it! Right now!"

He had expected to see his father rise from his chair and order the man out of his office. But instead he saw him sag in the chair, his face pale, his hands trembling. And then he started talking, rapidly, wildly, and in panic. He apologized. He apologized! He flattered and fawned, he agreed and promised to act quickly. And then he apologized again, said he was sorry for the misunderstanding, joked about it hollowly, and wound up shaking the man's hand and thanking him for his business. The man left with a sneer of triumph on his face.

Harry went back to his cage without speaking to his father and cashed the check. It was a gesture of defiance to his father,

83

his last in the banking business. That day was payday, and he drew his pay, emptied his checking account, hurried home and packed before his father arrived, and slipped out of the house.

At the railroad station he was at a loss about where to go, but just as he stepped up to the counter his eyes fell on a sign that said, "Baltimore and Ohio."

"A ticket to Baltimore," he said in a firm voice. "One way."

When he climbed down off the train the smell of the harbor was more than he could stand. It was like perfume from some exotic land and it drew him to the street that ran along the docks and slips. When he saw the activity and heard the sounds, and saw the tall masts of the sailing ships, he knew it was here that he must work. He saw a large black sailboat lying at a slip in front of him. He walked alongside and as he did a tall, weathered man came down the gangplank. "Excuse me, sir," he said. "I need a job. I don't know a damn thing about sailboats, but I'm strong and I'm willing to work."

Captain Talbott looked him over from head to toe. "What are you running away from?"

"My family, sir. They're trying to lock me up in a goddam bank."

That remark was met with a smile and there was a moment of silence. "Well, I am short a hand. You do look like a strong young man, and if you'll work,—have you any work clothes?"

"No sir, but I can get some in a hurry."

"Toby!" Another man, much younger, came up out of the cabin. "This is Mr.—what is your name, son?"

"Bailey, sir. Harry Bailey."

"This is Mr. Bailey. Mr. Bailey, meet Mr. Wheeler, the mate. Toby, take him ashore and help him find some work clothes. You have money to buy them, I suppose?"

"Yes sir."

"Yes, I thought you would. He'll be sailing with us this trip, Toby. This trip at least."

Well, it wasn't Mr. Bailey anymore. It was Harry, and he and Bull Shorter were the forecastle hands on the *Albatross*. It was hard work and it didn't pay much money, but Harry Bailey had found his place in the world and he knew that one day he would own a fleet of ships and sail them out of Baltimore to the ends of the earth. But first he had to learn the fundamentals.

Uncle John came up out of his cabin and closed the hatch behind him. The barometer had confounded him. Instead of continuing its steady rise, it had dropped back two tenths. He walked aft and lit the binnacle light and looked at the compass. It still indicated that north was where it had always been, but he wondered how long this would still be so. Nevertheless, for the present at least it was nice to know something had not gone crazy. And the wind was still north-northeast. He shook his head. "Goddamdest weather I ever saw," he said aloud.

He blew out the binnacle light and walked toward the gangplank. He saw a figure coming down the street out of the swirling snow. It was Tom Webster. He made no move to walk toward the *Albatross* and the two men met out in the open street in the manner of two men on their separate ways who chance to take intersecting paths. "I've been over to the other boats. No activity on any one of them. They're all secure and snug for the night, it looks to me. I'd say Billy Duke and Harry Marshall went on home like they said they were going to, but we'll take another look later on. Main thing we gotta do is get the hell away from here in case they're watching us. Where's your crew?"

"I think they're up the street getting dinner. Harry Bailey left here a while ago and he said he was going to meet the others. They weren't in the tavern so I assume they're at a place they eat at a lot of the time. It's just up the street and around the corner. I was about to go get them."

"Well, my boys are in the tavern over there and I broke the news to them and told them to stay where they were until about quarter past ten. I told them if they wanted to go home and get something that was all right, but not to go anywhere near the boat until then. I think you'd better do the same thing. Send 'em back to the tavern or tell 'em to go home for a while, but don't let 'em come aboard."

"Harry Bailey lives aboard, but I'll see if I can find them and keep them away. Oh hell, here they come now. Look at that, will you. The whole damn crew."

"All right. Don't get upset. Just take your cues from me. Tell them to come over here."

When the men got there, there were rapidly whispered instructions and then Captain Tom Webster turned and walked away. They all bid him good night, and Uncle John called after him, "See you in the morning, Cap'n Tom."

Tom Webster waved his arm without looking back and trudged on up the street. "All right now, Harry. Say good night and walk on aboard and go down in the foc'sle. After we leave, then you come up on deck and check the lines and then go back down again."

After Harry Bailey had gotten aboard the rest of them walked away. When they got to the corner Ed Shorter turned toward home, waving as he walked up the street, and Uncle John and Toby walked to the corner and turned in the direc-

86

tion of the Talbott house. The street was empty. There was no one at all left along the waterfront.

"Whatcha think?"

"I think exactly the same damn thing I've thought all along. I think that you, Billy Duke, are a damn fool."

"Look, I don't want him slippin' out of here tonight and gettin' the jump on me. He's done it too many times. And he said he was thinkin' about goin'."

"Oh for God's sake, Billy. You know him. You know what a joker he is. It was his idea of a joke, the whole damn thing. He never pulls anything simple. It's always involved and you never know it until he hits you with it. Now you know that."

"Sure. I'll admit it. But this don't sound like a trick to me."

"Oh hell, you just don't understand how his mind works. That man probably knows damn well we're freezing our asses off standing around here waiting to see what he's gonna do. And he probably hopes we'll stand here for another hour until the damn tide turns just to make sure he doesn't leave. Then tomorrow morning he'll laugh like hell at us, and even if we say we weren't he'll keep right on laughing, 'cause he'll know. He'll really know. You don't believe all that conversation was the truth, do you?"

"Well, what do you think?"

"Oh, I think it was real, all right. I think it was absolutely real. But it was an act. And I think he knew we were watching him and seeing the whole thing. I don't think he knew we were here in this doorway, but I think he knew we were someplace around close by, and the whole damn crowd of them were acting like they were trying to throw us off, but

87

being so damn obvious about it that we'd know they were fooling and would stay around here half the night. They're not going anyplace, Billy, nowhere except home to bed. And if we're smart we'll get out of this doorway and go home too."

"Maybe so, but what about Tom Webster? He must have been in on it too."

"Well sure he was. Hell, they probably thought this whole thing up a couple of days ago and decided to pull it on us tonight."

"Maybe you're right. It's a hell of a night for anything as stupid as going down the Bay anyway. All right. I guess you're right. He was foolin' us. All right. Let's give it up. Let's go on home. To hell with it."

The two men stepped out of the doorway and walked up the street. They turned the corner, looked back over their shoulders, saw no one, then went on. They walked rapidly for about three blocks, because it was cold and they wanted to get home, then came to a corner where their routes split. They said good night and Billy Duke crossed the street and walked straight ahead. Harry Marshall turned right, crossed the street, and began walking east. He walked a hundred yards and turned around. He came back to the corner and looked up the street. As far as he could see, which was not very far, there was no one. He turned south and headed back to the waterfront. In a few moments he was back in the doorway.

After about half an hour he felt cold. "I've got about a half an hour anyway," he thought. "I'll slip on down to the tavern and have me a little drink to warm me up, and then come back. While I'm there I'll tell my boys to stand by for a little while." He chuckled softly. "Even the third boat in will get a better price than the fourth. And poor old Billy Duke's home in bed by now."

At twenty minutes to ten he was back at his post in the doorway. He had only been there a minute when he saw someone coming down the street. He moved back into the shadows out of sight. Minutes passed. "I wonder what the hell happened to that man," he thought. He eased toward the edge of the doorway and peered around the corner. At that exact moment he saw the man. Saw him less than two feet away. And the man saw him at exactly the same moment. The next thing Harry Marshall knew he was falling backward into the doorway, lightning flashing before his eyes. He had not seen the man's fist coming, but he had felt it smash into his jaw. He felt his head hit the brick wall behind him, and that was the last thing he felt for quite a while.

The man, a huge, powerful, hard-faced boatswain off the *Western Belle,* the barque lying in the fairway, looked down at him. He was poised to kick him brutally in the face, but when Harry Marshall did not move he lowered his foot. He rubbed his right fist into the palm of his left hand. "That'll teach you to try to steal a man's hard-earned money, you miserable little small-town bastard."

Then he walked on, holding to the lee of the building, his arms tensed, his fists ready, his rolling gait stamping him as a deep water man off a mean ship.

Toby Wheeler was worried. As he and Uncle John walked back toward the wharf Toby was having a hard time making himself believe that this was really happening. He just couldn't believe they were really going to leave the harbor on such a night. They had never set sail on such a night in all the years he had been on the *Albatross.* It never occurred to

89

him to question the decision of his skipper, but he couldn't help but wonder why. In the ten years he had been aboard the *Albatross* he had never once felt any doubt about the wisdom of what John Talbott did.

Not that he had had the experience or the knowledge to question at the beginning, but now he did have, although the thought would never have occurred to him. There was more to it than just the relationship of master to mate. It went much deeper than that. There were certain loyalties and obligations to consider. For ten years Toby had been aboard the *Albatross* and she was his home. And in port, between trips, he had lived with the Talbotts, who had taken him off the streets when his mother died, and Laura Talbott had been more of a mother to him than his own.

He had come aboard at fifteen as an unneeded cabin boy, although he had not known this at the time. But as time passed and he grew older, he realized that the *Albatross* had never had a cabin boy before, and when he grew out of the job she was without one again.

The first day he came aboard the skipper had pointed out the fact that he would not always be a cabin boy, and had fired his imagination by telling him that he might someday be a Bay captain. And he had said something else that Toby had never forgotten. "Always remember this one thing when you get to be a captain. You are the captain because you can do any dirty, tough job on your boat better than any of your crew. And if you can, and they know you can, they will respect you and follow you anywhere, and you will never sail with an empty berth."

He had stood at the side of a master captain for ten years and because he was a bright youngster, he had watched, listened, and asked questions. And he had learned. He had learned to do every back-breaking task that came along and had learned to do them better than anyone else. And he had absorbed the lifetime of lore and knowledge stored in the mind of John Talbott.

At sixteen Toby began to do some of the work of a deck-hand. He learned to splice and crown quickly, and pulled his own weight on a halyard. A short time later he was standing a regular trick at the wheel. At twenty he was second mate, the first and last second mate on the *Albatross,* and he was handling the boat under way and making some of the landings. There was not a murmur of favoritism from the crew, and there was no doubt in his mind, or anyone else's, that he could handle the job when he was promoted to first mate when the job opened up.

It was a hard life, for the sea is a tough mistress, and a 90-foot schooner is demanding and unforgiving of even the slightest inattention, but as he looked back on it he knew that it had been wonderful and exciting too. There had been times when his labor left him exhausted, but there had never been a time when it had soured him. He had grown strong and wise in the ways of the Bay. He knew the pitfalls and the havens, the currents and the caprices of the weather. He was still a bit too young for command and he knew it, but he was a seasoned, valuable man who knew the day would come when he could rely on himself to exercise command.

"There must be something I don't understand," he thought. "Tom Webster says he's going and he's been sailing the Bay since the war."

He glanced at his skipper and cleared his throat. "Skipper, are we really going down the Bay tonight?"

"Why not?"

"Well, skipper, I don't know, but it seems like a hell of a

91

night, and I don't see a lot of other boats leaving port."

"Tom Webster's taking the *Hattie* out tonight. He's going along with us."

"He's really going, then?"

"That's right. We're going down together."

"How far are we going, skipper?"

"Solomons, if we can get in there. If we can't get in there we'll go to the mouth of the Potomac. Maybe the Rappahannock. I don't know. All depends on how it goes."

"Sure gonna be cold out there tonight, skipper."

"I know."

"Blowin' half a gale, too."

"I know."

"Snowin' a blizzard."

"I know."

"Did Captain Webster talk you into this, skipper? Tell you he felt this was a lucky night or something?"

"No, Toby. I talked him into it, I'm afraid."

"Skipper, would I be out of line if I asked why? Why tonight?"

"No. Mainly because I think the weather's gonna break. It's a chance to pick up a good profit at both ends. But, Toby, I was born and raised down there and I know a lot of those people. And I figure a lot of them are damn short of coal and some of them are cold. They're counting on somebody to get through to them soon or they'll be in real trouble. Maybe some of them already are. I think we ought to try, and I think this is the time to try."

Harry Bailey felt the first footfall on the gangplank, even though it was cushioned by snow. He hadn't really believed all the talk out in the street, he hadn't thought for one minute they would really go down the Bay. This was some sort of fancy joke someone was playing on someone else, although he wasn't quite certain as to what parties were actually involved. He hadn't gone quite so far as to pull off his outer clothing and climb into his bunk, but he was about to when he was aware of someone coming aboard the *Albatross*.

He tossed aside the reef point he was back-splicing and climbed the ladder out of the forecastle, shoved back the hatch, and came up on deck. He walked aft, peering through the snow, and made out the shape of John Talbott. Toby Wheeler was with him.

"Anybody else come aboard yet, Harry?"

"No sir, nobody else yet." He noted the expectancy in the skipper's voice. "My God," he thought, "maybe he really meant it."

"Well, Bull ought to be coming along pretty soon now."

"Are we sailing, skipper?"

"That's right. Now let's look alive and start getting ready to cast off. Here comes Bull now. Tide turns at 10:42 and we want to be ready for it."

"Yes sir." He watched Ed Shorter come up the gangplank.

"Hear that, Bull," Harry said. "We're getting ready to sail. We'll find out what kind of a sailor you are tonight. I'll bet you haven't seen anything like we're going to see tonight when you were rounding the Horn." He said it loud enough so John Talbott could hear it, and there was a note of reproach in his voice, but John Talbott had struck a match and was studying the thermometer on the binnacle, and if he heard it he gave no sign.

CHAPTER

5

"#8—Fresh gale—Breaks twigs off trees;
generally impedes progress—35 to 41 miles
per hour."
The Beaufort Scale of Wind Force.

"I'LL TELL you something, son. It wasn't an easy decision to make, and there was a time there when I think it kinda got out of my hands. I don't know whether I would have gone or not if it hadn't been that Tom Webster was pushing on me a little.

"But the time came and the crew was casting off and I could hear the crew on the *Hattie* doing the same thing, and well, by that time, son, there just wasn't any turning back.

"We cast off just as the boats began to swing around in the harbor. The ebb tide had just started to run as we drifted away from the wharf, but I'll tell you something, as we pushed off from the wharf and I took my hand away from that piling I was pushing on I felt like I had said goodby to the world for a while. It was a funny feeling, son. I just wanted to keep holding on to that pile all night long. I knew it was the last solid thing I was going to touch all night long."

94

At 10:42 the two schooners cast off and eased down the channel toward Seven Foot Knoll. Uncle John, standing beside the helmsman, watched the riding light of the *Shanghai Greyhound* fade into the gloom astern, then turned to peer forward through the snow, his eyes fixed on the lantern ahead. The *Hattie* had been moored a hundred feet downstream and she was leading the way.

Harry Marshall shook his head, reached up half conscious and felt his throbbing jaw. He was sitting in the doorway and it was several minutes before he realized what doorway it was and how he came to be there. But gradually it all came back, what had happened, why he was waiting in the doorway, and he could even understand what had prompted the man to lash out at him.

He lurched unsteadily to his feet and began walking across the street toward the row of slips and wharfs where the *Albatross* and *Hattie* were moored. Before he reached the other side of the street he could see the gaping hole in the forest of masts. The *Albatross* was gone. "That dirty son of a bitch!" he said. "He did it! He really did it!"

He ran down the wharf. There was another vacant berth and he knew that Tom Webster had gone too. He turned toward the tavern. "I'll show them," he shouted. "I'll show those two boys they can't get away with this!"

He was about to burst into the tavern shouting for his men when he realized what that might do. He stopped short, looked at his watch, and did a little figuring. 10:58. They must have just left. They were probably just out of sight in the snow. There was no use in alerting the entire waterfront. He walked quietly into the tavern and approached the three men in his crew, who sat at a table near the back of the room.

95

He slipped into a vacant chair. "They did it," he announced. "Tom Webster and John Talbott are gone. Just left, I reckon. Now let's get out of here quietly, ain't no use in attracting a lot of attention, and then let's get out of this harbor and go after those two sneaking bastards. They think they're so goddam great. We'll show 'em who can make a quick trip."

Jack Tighlman puffed on his cigar slowly and looked straight ahead. "We've been talking it over, Captain, and we don't think it's no fittin' night for us to be out."

Harry Marshall looked at them, every one of them, and not a one of them lowered his eyes.

"What the hell are you talking about? It ain't too bad a night for John Talbott's crew."

Jack Tighlman continued to look straight ahead. "That ain't us."

"Tom Webster's crew is out there too. It ain't too bad a night for them."

"That still ain't us."

"You mean you're refusing to sail with me tonight?"

Jack Tighlman nodded. "Ain't nothin' says we gotta sail with you tonight. Once we're on that boat we carry out your orders, but not here on shore. A man can always refuse to sail, and that's what we're doing."

"You're through. Every damn one of you."

"I reckon that's all right. I don't 'spect any one of us'll have trouble finding another berth."

"I'll double your shares on this trip."

"We're through. You just said so. Do you mind leavin', Captain Marshall. You're disturbing our drinking, sir."

Before the *Albatross* was fifteen minutes out a thin crust of snow had matted the front of Uncle John's heavy overcoat.

He beat at it with his hands and brushed it away. He turned to Harry Bailey, who was steering. "We'll change the helm every hour, Harry. Every hour on the hour. So you get a short trick to start. I'll take the wheel for a minute while you go tell Bull the news."

He took the wheel, wrapping his big fingers around the spokes, feeling the rudder kick against his hands. He looked aloft into the high rigging, wondering about the upper blocks and jaws of the main gaff, but he was unable to make out anything because of the darkness and snow. He studied intently the set of the big mainsail, paying particular attention to the area closest to the mast, searching for any flutter that might indicate luffing. It was set tight and drawing well. He nodded to Ed Shorter as he stepped to the wheel. "We have us a bird dog tonight, Bull." He pointed off to the lantern. "Stay with him. Follow that light."

An hour later, at exactly midnight, as though it had been geared in with the ship's clock striking eight bells, the wind suddenly freshened, the boat heeled to starboard, and the spray smashed back across the deck. It was cold, and it stung when it landed on the face. Uncle John turned and looked at Ed Shorter. Ed Shorter turned and smiled. It was a smile of pleasure. They had passed out from under the lee of North Point. They were now in the Chesapeake Bay and the welcome was not friendly.

At this precise moment, some fifty miles to the south, Seaman John Davis of the United States Coast Guard was climbing the spiral stairway to the top of the Cove Point Lighthouse. He was making a regularly scheduled check of the lens and its operating mechanism. When he reached the top of the stairs he stood for a moment gazing out at the fingers of light

97

that swept majestically around the lighthouse, each one sharply defined by the falling snow.

The lighthouse, a tall, circular, tapering white tower, stood on the western shore of the Chesapeake, at the mouth of the Patuxent River, on a point which, approaching from the north, makes well out into the Bay. To the south, the land falls away more gradually in a series of high bluffs, known as the Cliffs of Calvert, Calvert being the name of the county in which they are located. The station was manned by the Coast Guard and was a reporting station for ocean commerce inbound for Baltimore.

In addition to the lighthouse itself, which has been dear to the hearts of generations of Bay people, there was a large house for the light keeper, not a member of the Coast Guard, and his family. The house sat on concrete footings, protected by a sea wall and stone jetties, and was strongly made to withstand the winds that sweep down the Bay in the wintertime.

There was also a small shack located just to the south of the lighthouse, which housed the radio equipment, modest at that time, other signaling devices, and a long telescope used for the identification of ships passing up the Bay. There was also a barracks, off along the northern shoreline, for the single men of the Coast Guard who lived on the station. There were several married men in the complement at that time, but they lived off the station. All of these various buildings were connected by a series of walkways made of oyster shells, but none of them were visible on this night. The ground was completely covered with fourteen inches of snow.

Seaman Davis completed his check and went below to take over the mid-watch. As he trudged through the snow from the tower to the radio shack he was looking forward to a

98

quiet night. As far as he knew nothing was moving anywhere on the Bay. The *Shanghai Greyhound* had undoubtedly made Baltimore late in the afternoon. He had spoken to her before he turned over the watch the previous morning, and had reported her passage by telegraph to Baltimore.

The log bore out his conclusion. There had been no entries during the sixteen hours he had been off duty. He relieved the watch, who departed immediately for bed. The Coast Guard station was quiet. He was the only man on duty. He poured himself a cup of coffee and sat down to wait for 8:00 A.M.

Sails retrimmed, the *Albatross* wallowed in the heavy seaway for about twenty minutes before making another change in course. The spray still broke over the deck and at times the long bowsprit plunged into the sea, but the change in course gave the impression that the wind had slackened. The men relaxed ever so slightly. Uncle John took a turn around the deck to check the running tackle. A thin coat of ice was forming on everything and he put Harry Bailey to work breaking it away from blocks, windlasses, and halyards. A frozen block at a critical moment could be an expensive monument to carelessness, as he knew quite well, and Uncle John was not a careless man. He sailed his boat with skill and knowledge, relying on careful planning and long experience, leaving nothing to luck.

When others spoke of a mishap narrowly averted and praised their luck, he snorted and said that there was no such thing, that the man had just planned more carefully than he realized, or else he had reacted faster, that every time a man went to sea there were risks, and that careful planning and experience reduced these risks to a bare minimum. This was one of the reasons that he sailed this night with an experienced and devoted crew. There were few captains who were held in as high regard by their men. The rugged weather made it difficult enough to get good men for winter sailings, but add to that the slightest doubt in the skipper's seamanship, and his boat stayed in port.

In large measure this devotion of his men was the result of the devotion of the men who had sailed with him over the years. Their confidence in him had produced a confidence in himself. Their trust in him had produced a self-reliance and sureness that had fused into his personality. Thus he had come to believe, and not without good reason, that no matter what trials might beset him, with careful planning he could master them and would never be confounded.

He watched as Harry Bailey chipped away at the ice. He remembered that it was past the hour and was about to look for Toby to take the helm when he felt a hand on his shoulder. He turned and looked up at Ed Shorter. "Toby's got the wheel, skipper! Said he'd take it for the next hour! I'll help him!" He pointed at Harry Bailey.

Toby Wheeler felt a strange thrill go through him as the *Albatross* smashed her way through the waves. It was cold and raw, and downright uncomfortable to be out in weather like this, and if he had been ashore he would have thought twice about even stepping outdoors, but the liveness of it, the sounds and smells and movements, were so invigorating that the discomfort was very unimportant. He stood on the windward side of the wheel, his body leaning into the roll of the boat, his hands on the spokes, his head thrust forward on his neck as he studied the movements of the men on the deck, at the same time watching the set of the mainsail. "This is living," Toby Wheeler thought, and he was glad he had made up his mind to stay with the *Albatross* at least until after the first of the year.

The offer had come from the *St. Marys;* the second mate berth was open, and Captain Jimmy had assured him all he had to do was apply. But he had hesitated, and then decided to wait a little longer. He knew the time had come to give serious consideration to his career, but a man could miss life itself by worrying too much about his career. Maybe in the spring, even. That was time enough. "I'm glad I didn't miss this," he thought. He knew that the *St. Marys* was tied up back at Pier 8 and he was out on the Bay.

At 1:00 A.M. Toby was relieved. He had found that handling the *Albatross* in the heavy seaway called for sharpness and skill, and the weather wore hard on a man at the wheel, eroding his reflexes and sapping his strength to hold the boat on her course. He was surprised at how tired he was after the hour at the wheel. Cold he had known, and rough seas were nothing new, but the combination had a wearing effect that surprised him. He was happy to see Captain John come aft. He had been exposed to the same conditions, but at least he was able to move about, flap his arms and stomp his feet. But Toby had been a fixed target for the snow and icy spray as he stood poised and tense, rigidly holding the spokes of the wheel, his eyes fixed on the white lantern ahead. "All right, Toby. I'll take the wheel now. Go get Harry to relieve you."

In a moment Harry Bailey came up to take the wheel. "Follow that lantern on the *Hattie's* stern," Uncle John said as he turned over the wheel.

"Yes sir. Sure is a hell of a night, isn't it?"

"It is for a fact, Harry. I've never been out on a worse one, and for sure I never set out on a night like this before. But I think we'll see the sun in the morning, boy. I truly do."

Seaman John Davis looked up at the clock. The time was dragging. He had only had the watch for an hour and five minutes, but it seemed like all night. He was deep in the study of "The Elements of Navigation," by W. J. Henderson. Davis was an ambitious young man who hoped to make a career of the Coast Guard service, and he studied constantly to improve his knowledge. He had been working with this book for quite some time, and felt that he had absorbed a large amount of its complex detail. At times he had been able to borrow a sextant and take observations of the sun, which had worked out surprisingly well. He re-read the paragraph in front of him. "Remember that you can never be too sure of your position. Eternal vigilance is the price of safety at sea, and dangers increase with the approach to land."

His roommate, until recently stationed at Cape Hatteras, was full of stories that were testimony as to the accuracy of this statement. Also, he remembered reading of the Spanish steamer, *Principe de Asturias*, striking a rock off Sebastien Point in the spring with the loss of 500 lives.

CHAPTER

6

"Speaking very generally, it is time to reef
whenever you first begin to feel like it."
From *The Amateur Seaman*,
by H. S. Smith.

"AND I REALLY thought we would see the sun in the morning.
It seemed like a wild sort of thing to say out there then, with
the snow coming down and the wind blowing like that, but I
thought I had it figured out and besides, I had a feeling in
my bones. When you've been on the Bay as long as I had, you
develop a very sensitive set of bones, boy. They tell you all
sorts of things. And my bones were telling me we were in for
a change in the weather, and a change for the better."

"It must have made it a lot easier having Tom Webster's
light to follow out there on a night like that," I said.

"Well now, yes and no. Oh, it was a comfort all right to
know there was somebody in the world who was as big a fool
as I was, and it was good to know that he thought we were
headed in the right direction too. But let me tell you something, son. When you're following somebody else, it's always
a good idea to know where you are going. Because if you lose

him, or if he begins to go astray, at least you know where you are. In a lot of cases even if you don't know where you are, as long as you know how you got there you have a chance of getting back. Although I can't say we would have had much chance of getting back into Baltimore harbor that night."

But the temptation was great, with the ice and snow distracting him, for Uncle John to simply say "follow that light," without regard for his own navigation. Others would probably have done just that, but the price of losing Captain Tom Webster in the storm, without knowledge of his own position, was too horrible to risk. To be suddenly cut off from everything if that light vanished in the snow, with no landmark to use as a departure point, would make his position impossible to ascertain. So, regularly he went below, consulted his clock, chart, and parallel rules, arriving at a position based on dead reckoning, plus a certain amount of God and guess.

Immediately after Harry Bailey took the wheel, Uncle John went below and began his computations on the long shelf in his cabin. Tide about so much, give or take a little because of the wind pushing at the water, course about so much, since it was impossible to steer a precise course in such heavy weather, and time, exactly for a change, so much. With these estimates he drew his course line on the chart, and using his dividers, ticked off the miles, hoping for compensating errors that would somehow balance out instead of errors that would compound the slightest miscalculations in the process into one huge catastrophe that would cast him ashore.

This bit of mental gymnastics was done each time the course was changed, or each hour, if the course was maintained that long. As he stepped back on deck at 1:10 he looked off to port into the snow as if he expected by some miracle to see the light at Love Point, which they were passing at this moment, according to his calculations.

By this time the bow of the *Albatross* was pointed straight down the Bay. The wind was far around on the port quarter and the boat was yawing and pitching, her tall masts inscribing great circles in the ceiling of snow. It was snowing much harder; the wind screamed through the frozen rigging, and the sickening lurch that came with each overtaking wave left little doubt that the storm was mounting in fury. The wind was almost straight out of the north now, and very close to a whole gale. Uncle John was very glad he had come out of Baltimore with a double reef in the mainsail, stowed foresail, and the bonnet out of the jib.

Her bow was now plunging into every wave, and at times he feared that she would be driven under. Rivers of water poured astern each time her bow came up. Some of it ran down the deck and poured out the scuppers. Some of it froze to the lower rigging. And some of it formed a thin sheet of ice on the deck. It was extremely hazardous to move about. Snow was sticking to everything. Uncle John wondered how the crew of the *Hattie* was standing up to the tortures of the night.

When the two boats had changed course near Baltimore Light, the *Albatross* had been riding about thirty yards aft on the port quarter of the *Hattie,* but on the reach that followed, with her centerboard raised slightly, she had drawn up inch by inch until she was now directly abeam, with a scant twenty yards separating the two schooners. Uncle John could see the *Hattie's* port running light, a diffused red glow, rising and falling through the snow. He could hear the crushing rush of water between the two boats.

He considered the fact that he was gradually gaining on

her and was pleased with this knowledge, knowing the *Alba-tross'* speed would stand him in good stead on the way home. He hoped the *Hattie* was also sailing with her board partly raised, since this would be the only way to compare the two boats, and he was sure she was. He couldn't imagine Tom Webster not taking advantage of the following wind in this manner. He took the wheel and told Harry Bailey to go below and lower the board slightly. He didn't aim to pass Captain Webster and the *Hattie* and lose them in the night.

He knew clearly in his mind what his action would be upon reaching the mouth of the Patuxent. He would be almost up under the stern of the *Hattie* at that time, maybe a little to port, with his crew ready. He would figure it as fine as he could, attempting to get the jump on the *Hattie's* crew, then jibe under her stern, blanket her wind as he passed her, slip around Drum Point, and run for Cook's wharf, taking the inside channel, beating the *Hattie* to the dock, and unloading immediately. It would have to be a fast operation, and he hoped he could get a wharf crew working with him before Tom Webster came in. Loose coal was always slower to unload than barrels of coal oil.

He knew that even if the two boats got away to an even start back from Solomons he had the faster boat. He knew from the past that she pointed higher and was faster on the wind, and now he was seeing that she sailed faster off the wind. He only hoped he had the skill to overcome Tom Webster's experience and cunning. He knew it would be a boat race all the way up the Bay.

When Harry Bailey returned to the wheel Uncle John walked along the lee railing, eyeing the length of the main boom, inspecting the ties of the reef points. All seemed to be well tied and none seemed to be showing any sign of stress.

He looked aloft at the set of the main gaff, and grasping a handrail along the edge of the cabin truck, he looked far aloft into the rigging, not really being able to distinguish anything, but it was a look that followed his thoughts, which were up there in that rigging wondering if any of the blocks were jammed and frozen. There was no way to tell at this point, unless he wanted to drop the sails, and he didn't want to find out that badly. He didn't dare send a man up the mast in this kind of weather, either.

"Everything all right, skipper?"

He looked around and saw Ed Shorter standing next to him. "I'm just wondering about those blocks up there. Wondering if any of them are frozen."

"I'll go up and see if you want me to."

"Be a hell of a trip up there and back, Bull."

"Yes sir. But I don't think you have to worry none, skipper. Not as long as it's snow that's fallin', anyhow. If this stuff was to turn to rain with the temperature below freezing like it is then we'd really have ourselves a problem. But it seems to me like the main problem is always with the line freezin' before anything like that happens. When that happens it don't make no difference if you can run it through the blocks or not. Movin' around seems to help, though. All that stuff pullin' and haulin' around up there don't give it too much chance to set up unless it gets real cold. Main thing you gotta worry about is something pulling loose when everything gets froze up. But that's all good tackle up there. I looked at it the other day."

"The hell you did!"

"Yes sir. I didn't have nothin' else to do, so I climbed up there and looked it over. I was pretty jumpy the other day. The old lady was giving it to me at home about touchin' up

107

the livin' room woodwork before the holidays, and hell, I had to do something. Sometimes I wonder why a man like me ever gits himself married to begin with. Anyway, all that tackle up there is in good shape."

Uncle John always thought Bull Shorter was something wonderful. He grinned and shook his head slowly. He reached over and put his hand on the Bull's shoulder. "Bull," he said, "it is a pleasure to have a real sailor like you on board. You've spoiled me pretty bad, though. I didn't even think of checking that rigging before we left and with a man like you on board I guess I don't have to."

"Thank you, sir, but I wouldn't say this crew's exactly short on real sailors. Any one of 'em could have shipped out deep-water and not got hisself lost."

"I know. I'm damned lucky to have a crew as good as this one."

"And it's a damn good thing to have 'em on a night like this too, ain't it, sir?"

John Talbott nodded. He looked up at the mainsail. "I reckon we could ease that main sheet a little, Bull. Wind seems to be working around to the north'rd." He leaned forward as if to see the jib better. "You get the jib sheet and I'll take care of the main. After that why don't you go below and warm yourself. Harry and I can watch her for a while."

Ed Shorter worked his way forward along the slippery deck, always braced, always ready to be knocked off balance, always looking at the object he would grab for if he felt himself beginning to slip. When he reached the deck cleat holding the jib sheet he stopped and loosened the sheet line. He paid out the line slowly. He was facing aft, his right foot against the forward end of the cleat, thus bracing himself, and letting the line slide around the aft end of the cleat, leaning slightly forward against the pull of the line and looking over his shoulder at the jib, which was a vague white shape forward. He paid out the line hand over hand, listening intently, trying to catch the first sound of flapping that would tell him he had eased the sail a little too much.

When he heard it, and felt it slightly in his fingers, he took in slightly on the line, sheeted it home, and took a hitch around the cleat. He stood up, reached out and grabbed the handrail on the top of the forecastle roof, and stood for several moments savoring the night. "This is truly living," he thought. Normally he would not have said anything so fancy as that, but once, when he had shipped out on a deep-water barque running from New York to Valparaiso for a load of nitrate, he had heard a very proper New England captain use that phrase on a starry night in the southern latitudes. The ship was bowling along at about twelve knots on an easy passage down toward the roaring forties, but she had not gotten there yet, and was still in the warm, lush air of the South Atlantic.

Actually, that had not really been Ed Shorter's idea of truly living, but as the ship got down to fifty degrees south of the Line, and the air got bitter and the seas became mountainous, she approached the area that he thought was the only place on earth where there was "truly living." To Ed Shorter the passage of Cape Horn was the supreme moment in life. To him the fact that he was a man who regularly doubled the Horn was the most important single thing that life could offer. He relished the violence, thrilled to the perils, and came to life out of a quiet state of watchful waiting when he knew the ship had passed fifty south.

He knew men who hated the Horn, he knew captains who were terrified of the passage, he knew captains who had been

109

turned back after days of grueling work climbing up the westerly gales, mainly because they were, in this area, timid men, afraid to carry the sail necessary to conquer the seas and the winds around the Horn. And he had also known captains who gave up at the first opposition and ran all the way around the globe at fifty south, at the bottom of the world, to come to their destination, even if it was up the west coast of South America.

But he had also known and sailed with captains who regarded the challenge of the Horn as the supreme test, for he had sailed on the great barques of the Flying "P" Line of the House of Laeisz of Hamburg, Germany. He had first shipped out on one of their ships after he had jumped an American ship in Valparaiso because of the food and because of the abuse the crew took from the captain and the bucko mates. He found a berth in the *Plus,* and she was a ship to his liking. The food was good and the men got good treatment. He soon discovered that this was a characteristic of all Laeisz ships, and he found that the ships made fast runs. He knew by heart the first words in the instructions to each master of a Laeisz ship. "My ships can and shall make *fast* voyages." The instructions were signed by "F. Laeisz," and his ships did make fast voyages.

He later served in the *Potosi,* a mighty five-masted barque, made of steel, rigged with wire and chain, expertly sailed by the greatest of all Laeisz masters, Robert Hilgendorf, a man who believed implicitly the instructions of his owners. On one voyage he sailed the *Potosi* from the English Channel to Valparaiso in 55 days!

In 1901 Ed Shorter had shipped out of Hamburg for Baltimore, and after twenty years on Laeisz ships, for the first time he came back home. When he saw the land of his birth after so long a time away he was overwhelmed with a longing to stay ashore for a while and renew old acquaintances. Because hands were easy to find for Laeisz ships, and because of his long and faithful service, he was allowed to sign off the ship in Baltimore, was paid off, and two days later he watched the ship sail away down the Patapsco.

Within a week he was wandering about the waterfront looking for a ship bound for Hamburg; a Laeisz ship preferably, a German ship if possible, but under no circumstances did he consider shipping out on an American ship. He had the opportunity, because at the end of the second week ashore an American ship did sail for Hamburg, but Ed Shorter was not on her. He didn't like the look of her. She was hogged and had a mean look. In addition he heard that her skipper was a tyrant.

At the end of the third week ashore, at a loss to do anything constructive about getting to sea, he got married. He hadn't planned to get married, he hardly knew the girl he married, but he didn't marry her because he was drunk, he wasn't tricked, and he knew exactly why he was doing this thing which to him was earth-shaking. He did it because he was powerless to do anything else. At one moment he was drifting free in a pleasant but rudderless state, and the next he was crowding sail in a headlong pursuit, knowing full well the course he had taken and what lay ahead at the end of the pursuit.

She was a pretty girl, the widow of a young Cape Horner gone missing, and the difference in their ages was astonishing. She was twenty-two and he was forty-eight. She saw in him a great big, lovable, tender protector and provider who was very much a man, and he saw her as a demanding, strong-minded young woman who was also very much a fascinating, captivating little witch, giving her rewards as freely and as frequently as she made her demands, but never with any calculated relation between the two. She took advantage of him atrociously, but lovingly; she ran his life tenderly, and with his welfare always uppermost in her mind, but she ran it nevertheless; and he loved every minute of it no matter how loudly he protested to his fellow crew members.

She never heard his protests, although she would have laughed them off and loved him a little more, understanding the reason for them. He never complained to her. He wouldn't have dared, although he certainly wasn't physically afraid of the wrath of such a slip of a girl. He was still completely unable to understand his good fortune in having won her, and he was constantly waiting for the bubble to burst, and thus he was afraid to raise his voice against her slightest whim. In addition, he was thrilled every time she offered him a chance to do some little thing to make her happy, no matter how outrageous it might be.

But since a man couldn't admit these feelings to his shipmates, he constantly pictured himself as a man beset and besieged from the moment he set foot on dry land until the time he left it. No one who had ever seen the two of them together believed a single word of it, but they all humored him because to argue was to admit jealousy.

From the first she put her foot down on any idea of shipping out deep water again, but she raised no objection when he announced that he had signed on the *Albatross*. In fact, it seemed to Ed that she was quite pleased with the way it had worked out. She always seemed to enjoy the flurry of excitement as he dressed to leave for the *Albatross*. She stayed very close to him on sailing days, teasing him about having to play second mate to a sailboat, and accusing him of being glad to get rid of her and return to his first love. Each goodby left him with a warm, satisfied feeling, and he went back to his work relaxed and steady, content with his new way of life.

She was always watching from the window as he came striding eagerly up the street, hurrying home to her at the end of every trip. And when they were together she made love to him in a way that lifted his spirits to heights he had only known on the fore-royal yard, shortening sail before a howling blast of wind. He could never put it into words to tell her, but she had become life itself to him, the kind of "truly living" he had known only on the footrope, bending over the royal yard, swinging like an inverted pendulum above the rolling deck, fisting the big sail in, muzzling it, and securing it with gaskets, gale winds roaring and pounding at his back, and rain, sometimes sleet, blowing almost horizontally past him. Such was the splendor of the way she loved him.

At first Bay sailing seemed tame to him, but it wasn't long before he had changed his mind. His first winter convinced him it offered the challenge his spirit demanded. By the time spring came to the Chesapeake he knew he had picked a good boat, good shipmates, and a skipper who would sail when many others stayed in port. After the years on Laeisz ships, this was the type of skipper he was used to.

He looked aft along the pitching, yawing deck of the *Albatross,* now completely white with snow. He studied the tightly furled foresail to make certain none of the canvas was working loose from its stops. He looked at the big double-reefed mainsail. It was all they could possibly carry and he silently praised his skipper's judgment. A less prudent man would have been faced with the messy and dangerous task of shortening sail under extremely hazardous conditions, and a more cautious man would have stayed in port, probably without so much as a thought of going out on such a night.

Ed Shorter knew that most captains he had sailed with would have been down to topsails and staysails by now, if the weather conditions had been comparable. There was nothing weak or tender about the *Albatross*. She could carry it, and there was certainly nothing timid about her skipper. They were not in port, and he was proud of that.

The jib was drawing well, so he made his way aft, carefully rounding the afterend of the forecastle house, already anticipating with great relish the warmth of the coal stove below. He had sailed on ships where there was never a fire in the forecastle, no matter what the weather. He opened the double doors, but instead of sliding back the hatch cover grabbed the handles on top with both hands, pulled himself off the deck in a suspended crouching position, swung his feet over the ledge, straightened his legs, and put his feet on the top step of the ladder going down into the cabin. He arched his back and twisted his head sideways, pulling it in under the hatch cover. He turned around and pulled the doors shut. The sound of the wind faded, but he could hear the sound of the water rushing by the bow quite clearly. He could hear the dull crash each time the bow smashed into a wave.

Harry Bailey saw the glow of light forward as the forecastle doors opened, he saw the silhouette of Ed Shorter's body framed in the light, then watched the light go out as the doors closed. "Christ, I'm cold," he thought.

Toby Wheeler steadied himself against the roll of the boat and carefully poured himself a cup of coffee. He was standing in the galley, such as it was, which was on the starboard side of the after cabin, just forward of the captain's quarters. It was a very small room, large enough for a coal stove that was ample for the meals cooked on board during trips, an ice box, storage space for staples, and a sink. The sink had a pump that pumped in sea water, which was used for washing dishes, and when the stopper was pulled the water ran down a scupper back into the sea. The galley was the province of Harry Bailey, who did all the cooking for the crew.

The galley was separated by a counter from the area where the crew ate. The eating area, which had no formal name, was never called anything in particular by the crew. It was certainly not called the dining saloon, or the ward room, or anything else that might serve as a title on a larger ship. This area formed the forward half of the after cabin.

To enter it, a man came down the after steps, walked along the passageway between the captain's cabin and that of the first mate, and on into the room. It had one window in the forward part of the cabin trunk and two on the port side. There were also two windows in the galley on the starboard side. All of these windows were tightly sealed and never opened. The ventilation came from two scoop-shaped funnels that went up through the ceiling and were turned one way or the other, depending on the weather and whether or not it was necessary to keep out the spray or rain or snow, in which case their openings were turned away from the wind. They were turned with their faces toward the breeze if the breeze was cool and dry. There was also a skylight, directly over the middle of the room, and this was opened in good weather.

Toby took a sip of the steaming black coffee he had poured for himself and made a face at the taste of it. He knew it wasn't bad coffee, but he knew it didn't taste good to him, and he felt that at this moment nothing would taste very good. He had been in the cabin for upward of twenty minutes making that pot of coffee, and the longer he stayed the more he was conscious of the heat and the stuffiness. It was the same feeling he had experienced in the tavern before they sailed, the feeling that had gone away once they left and got outside in the fresh air. His stomach was unsettled again and he could feel himself beginning to sweat, particularly across the forehead. He took another sip of coffee, then turned the cup and poured the rest of it down the drain of the sink. He put the coffee pot in a box-like base on the counter so it wouldn't go sliding around, tossed his tin cup in the sink, and then headed for the deck. The need for a breath of fresh air was overwhelming.

Ed Shorter looked up at the lantern swinging from the middle of the forecastle ceiling. Its very motion seemed to disturb him. It seemed to aggravate the strange feelings he was experiencing in his stomach. The air in the forecastle was hot and stuffy. The coal stove had been allowed to get out of hand, he thought, noticing that the damper at the bottom was open. He slid off his bunk and staggered over and closed it, then opened the upper door. Once his feet were on the deck he realized that the movement of the boat was not the only thing that was causing him to be unsteady. He turned and lurched back to his bunk. He threw himself up into it and rolled over on his back. He looked straight up at the ceiling above him, carefully avoided the swinging lantern. "Christ," he said aloud, "I'm not seasick. I never been seasick in my whole life. My guts are sure settin' in for a storm though. I feel like I'm gonna puke all over the goddam place. Maybe I can make it up on deck and get some fresh air."

He rolled off the bunk and tried to stand, but just as he did the *Albatross* lurched and skittered and he went to his hands and knees. That same moment a wave of violent nausea hit him. It was uncontrollable. An explosion came bursting up through his throat. He tried to throttle it, but it continued to come surging up and when it found his teeth were clenched and his lips were tightly closed it flooded into the back of his nasal passage and pushed on until it was running from his nostrils, forcing him to open his mouth. At the same time he felt the beginnings of a dizziness he had never known before, heard a keen whining in his ears, and felt himself begin to move in great looping circles, until it all suddenly ceased and he knew nothing.

Toby Wheeler ducked through the after companionway doors, closed them behind him without looking back, and took a deep breath of fresh air. He took another, and felt the mounting nausea begin to go away. He looked around, dismayed by the change that had taken place on deck in the twenty-five minutes he had been below making coffee. She was a floating drift of snow, or so it seemed. She had the shape of a boat, but none of the details of her rigging, running tackle, or deck gear showed as such. All of it took on a fuzzy shape, and the windlasses, cleats, and chocks were only small mounds of snow. He looked around for Captain John, wondering where he could be, then saw him as he straightened up from sheeting home the mainsail. He walked over to him, meeting him coming toward the wheel, and the two men stood for several seconds looking at each other. "Snowing, ain't it, skipper?"

"It damn sure is, Toby. Harder than it was when we left the slip. A lot harder, I'd say, but maybe it's just that the wind is driving it so hard."

"It wasn't sticking to her like it is now. Not half an hour ago it wasn't."

"I know. I wonder when it's going to stop."

"I wonder if it's going to stop!"

"I know."

"*Hattie's* still in sight, I see." Toby saw the light, more of a glow than a light in the snow, just forward off the starboard bow.

"Yep, and I hope to God she stays in sight. It's a comfort to know she's there. Reminds me there's someone else who's as big a fool as I am."

"Also someone who thinks we're on course. Don't forget that, skipper. Where do you think we are, by the way?"

"Well, I figure we passed Love Point about—" he leaned around and looked at the clock in the binnacle housing— "about thirty-five minutes ago."

"Makin' good time, ain't we?"

"We oughta be. We've got everything in our favor. Wind fair and blowing a gale and the tide still ebb. We oughta be making time. I only hope we can stop when the time comes."

The two men laughed and Toby turned away. He walked to the after cabin trunk, felt through the snow until he felt the handle of a heavy, wide, stiff bristle push broom. He untied the stop cords holding it in place and began to push the snow across the deck, shoving it toward the lee rail. Each wide swath he cleared showed an undercoating of ice. He stopped. He struggled back across the deck, the broom still in his hand. "I think it might be better to just leave it, skipper. It's better footing than the ice."

Captain John said nothing. He pointed toward where Toby had been sweeping. There was no ice any more. It was covered with snow already. Toby nodded and replaced the broom on the cabin trunk.

"There's coffee fresh made below, skipper. I'll take her for a while. Why don't you go down and warm up for a few minutes and have you a cup."

Toby watched him nod, walk toward the hatch, then disappear below. He walked to the binnacle, checked the course, then stepped back. "Hell of a night, ain't it, Harry?"

"I've never been so cold in my life, Mr. Wheeler."

"Well, you're better than halfway through your trick. It's warm down in the forecastle, and it won't be too long before you're down there. Think about that. Maybe it'll warm you up a little."

Harry Bailey nodded and said nothing.

Captain John was below for fifteen minutes. When he came back on deck Toby noticed he had put on dry clothing and another suit of oil skins. He was smoking a fresh cigar. He checked the compass and clock, nodded to Toby, and said, "I've got it, Toby. Please go forward and tell the Bull to get ready to relieve the wheel. Tell him to put on all the warm clothing he's got."

Toby eased his way forward, fighting every inch of the way to keep from slipping and falling to the deck. He knew that if he did he would slide all the way to the lee rail, and then maybe he'd catch himself and maybe he wouldn't. He opened the doors to the forecastle, swung himself through, and climbed halfway down the ladder. He stopped short. "What the hell's the matter down here, Bull?"

Ed Shorter was on his hands and knees, crawling across the deck toward his bunk. He looked up with glassy eyes. His face was ashen and his jaw hung slack. As his eyes took in this scene, Toby's nose took in the foul smell of the forecastle. He began to comprehend what had happened.

119

He watched Ed Shorter try to speak, then shut his mouth tightly. Toby watched his cheeks puff out until it seemed they would explode. And suddenly, it was as if they had. Toby leaped down the last three steps of the ladder. He straddled Shorter and hooked his hands under his stomach, lifting with each convulsion in an attempt to ease his struggle.

"Those oysters," Toby thought. "Those goddam oysters."

Suddenly he felt the nausea returning. He could feel its first beginnings as it moved on him. He knew he had to get out of the forecastle, out on deck, out of this stinking hole, or he would be finished. Ed Shorter was sagging in his arms, his knees just off the floor, his head down almost as if his neck were broken. Toby began to shift him over toward the bunks on the starboard side, but he knew he was not going to be able to hold out that long. He eased the unconscious man down onto the deck and bolted for the ladder. He fought his way up and out into the open air. He left the doors open, hoping the fresh air would have a good effect on the Bull.

As he worked his way aft along the windward side of the boat he felt his control returning. By the time he reached the wheel he knew he was not going to vomit, at least not for the time being, although he still felt slightly unsteady on his feet, but even that was going away.

It wasn't until he came around the corner of the after cabin trunk that he began to realize the full import of the message he was about to deliver. All thought of telling Captain John about his own condition faded. He couldn't get sick, not now. There were only three men now. Three out of four, and one of them, himself, not really up to the struggle that he knew was coming. "Well," he thought, "I'll just have to be."

"Gonna be a long night!" he shouted.

"What's the matter?"

"Ed Shorter's sick down there!"

"Sick! The hell he is!"

"The hell he ain't! Sicker'n anybody you ever saw!"

"What's the matter with him!"

"Food poisoning! Sicker'n hell. Threw up all over the foc'sle!"

"Food poisoning?"

"Yes sir! We all ate dinner at the same place! Had oysters! Must have been spoiled! Only thing I can figure!"

"Did you eat them?"

"Yes sir!"

"Did you eat those oysters, Harry?"

"Yes sir!"

CHAPTER

7

"Remember, Lord, my ship is small and
thy seas are so wide!"
An old fisherman's prayer.

CAN YOU imagine what a crushing blow it must have been to
Uncle John when he suddenly found that he was without the
most experienced member of his crew? Can you possibly imagine? Not only that, but to know he was also in immediate
danger of losing the other two as well. Can you possibly imagine what it was like to learn of this crushing twist of fate
standing on the rolling deck of a crashing, pounding 90-foot
schooner, with a wild winter gale of snow blowing at your
back and your boat sailing very close to the limits of human
control, and just as close to taking things into her own hands
and ending your life? What would you have done? First?

"There's no use crying about it, son. There's nothing to be
gained by standing there wringing your hands and shouting,
'Woe is me!' If there's one thing you learn on the water it is
that. Things keep going on. Nothing stops. The waves never
stop, the tide keeps right on running. You have to make up
your mind what you are going to do and then do it. A lot of

122

thoughts went through my mind when Toby told me that, but all my thoughts were about just one thing and how to do it best."

If you had been Uncle John, the first thing you would have done, first before all else, would have been to take care of Bull Shorter. There was no hesitation, no standing helpless, no wondering what to do, no cursing the fates that had so badly betrayed him.

"I'm going forward, Toby! Got to see what I can do for the Bull. Stay up here in the fresh air! And for God's sake, keep that lantern in sight! We can't lose it now!"

So he went forward to take care of the man who was sick. Toby was right, it was going to be a long night, maybe even longer than he could imagine. A trip to the mouth of the Potomac no longer seemed a remote possibility. It was more of a probability. It seemed essential not to abandon Bull to his misery although he knew there would be little immediate effect regardless of what he did. But he must do something, not only because he was part of his crew, but because he needed him and must do all he could to restore him to a useful state as quickly as possible.

He needed him very badly right now, but that was out of the question. Later there would be an even greater need, and he must attempt to do what he could with his scant medical knowledge and limited supplies. He knew the illness probably would not be fatal, that it would run its course and the Bull would recover in time, even if he did nothing, but if he could treat him and shorten the period of time he would be sick, well, it was worth a try.

He wanted to see the Bull for himself before he made up his mind what he could do for him, so he worked his way along the deck toward the forecastle without stopping in his own cabin for medicine. As he went he noticed that all around him the snow and ice were getting thicker on the running gear. With two men remaining on deck and one below, he realized that unless he chipped it off himself it would just have to stay there. Another factor had been added to the relentless equation that was becoming more and more unbalanced against him.

The stench rocked him as he swung in through the open companionway and went down the ladder. He saw Ed Shorter, still on the deck, apparently unconscious, spread-eagled, his face lying in a fresh mess of vomit.

He dropped off the ladder and went to pick him up. He heaved him up off the floor. It was all he could do to move him, and he almost lost his footing several times on the slimy deck before he wrestled the big, limp body over near the bunk. He spread him out on a clean spot and pulled off his sea boots, stripped off the wet oilskins, pulled down the covers, then lifted him up into the upper bunk, shoved him under the covers, and tucked the blankets up around his chin.

"I'm going for medicine now, Bull," he said, although he doubted that the man heard him. "I'll be back as soon as I can."

He climbed the ladder and returned aft across the treacherous deck. The snow beat into his face as he went, but the cold fresh air felt good, driving the smell of the forecastle out of his head. As he rounded the end of the after cabin trunk he waved at Toby and Harry. Toby waved back, but Harry Bailey was too busy fighting with the wheel to take his hand off the spokes.

As he came into the cabin he looked up at the clock over the chart table. 2:04. For the first time since he had heard

124

about the sick man he stopped to make a choice. The hour had passed without a position report in the log. That should be done, since he knew it might be the last one he would make in hours. He had to know where he was, or at least where his dead reckoning showed him to be, and the more current the position the better. If he lost the *Hattie* in the snow it would be the only thing he had to go on.

But the Bull needed attention. The forecastle needed cleaning. He could not possibly recover in that stinking place. He didn't stop to think about who would swab down the deck. He knew who would do it. He would do it. He looked at the medicine cabinet on the bulkhead. He looked at the chart table, and again at the clock. He had wasted one precious minute trying to make up his mind.

He took a deep breath and walked to the chart table. This had to be, he thought, but he knew it wouldn't take long and it would be very important.

He took his parallel rules and pencil and began to mark off his course. Then he took the dividers and spread them along the closest meridian. He measured off the proper number of minutes of latitude, each minute representing one nautical mile, then moved the dividers over to the course line he had drawn, put one point on the last estimated position, and stuck the other point through the paper further along the line. He took the pencil and marked an "X" over the dot on the chart. He wrote "2 A.M." alongside it. His eyes swept the area around the "X," taking in the points of land and where they lay, the shoals and markers, and it was almost as if he were on deck on a clear day looking out over the water. If he was indeed where his dead reckoning showed him to be, then he was completely familiar with his surroundings. He knew exactly where he was, and he knew how it would look if there were no snow or restricted visibility.

He snapped the dividers closed, picked up the rules and the pencil, tossed them all in the drawer and closed it. He turned and opened the medicine cabinet. He puffed on his extinguished cigar as he examined the contents. Then he reached up and pulled down a package of Dover's Powder. Things would get a hell of a lot worse before they got any better, but if there was anything left in their stomachs this would get it out, and it would sweat some of it out too. There was nothing else that looked like it might do the job. He was not exactly prepared for this type of illness. He was more prepared for cuts and bruises. He shook out a half a dozen of the small paper envelopes and put them on the chart table.

He stopped in the galley and drew a pail of fresh water from the tank. He shoved a tin cup in one pocket and the box of Dover's Powder in another. This way he could carry the water bucket in one hand and still have the other hand free to fend for himself as he crossed the icy deck. He climbed the ladder and as he came out through the companionway he tossed a quick look over his shoulder to starboard. The lantern was still out there in the snow.

When he came down the forecastle ladder this time he saw that Ed Shorter had come to sufficiently to have his eyes open. He watched as the man shifted his eyes and slowly turned his head as he approached the bunk. "I ain't ever been seasick before," he said weakly.

"You aren't seasick. Those oysters you had for supper were spoiled. How do you feel?"

There was an almost imperceptible shake of the head. "Not so good," he mumbled.

"I've got something here that'll fix you up." Uncle John braced himself against the roll of the boat, filled the tin cup

126

with water, and dissolved three of the powders in the water. "Open your mouth."

When the medicine was in his mouth he closed his eyes and sighed. After that Uncle John washed his face with fresh water and set out to clean up the mess on the forecastle deck. He knew he could not risk exposing Toby or Harry to the smell. He wanted to keep them up in the fresh air. He took the draw bucket full of foul water topside and heaved it over the side, rinsed it out, then returned below with fresh sea water. He swabbed the deck, emptied the dirty water again, and went below to rinse the deck. When he had finished he set the bucket of rinse water by the ladder, stowed the mop, and turned his attention to Ed Shorter again. He was asleep and Uncle John saw with satisfaction that he seemed to be breathing easily. He paused for a moment to feel his pulse and was about to turn and leave to go back to the after deck when he heard a noise behind him and whirled around just in time to see Harry Bailey come staggering down the ladder and collapse in a heap on the deck.

Ed Shorter opened his eyes and rolled his head so he could see what was happening. He looked out over the rim of the bunk and saw Harry Bailey lying on the deck with the skipper standing over him. "Oh Christ!" he thought. "That makes two of us. That don't leave nobody on the deck but Toby. Why the hell did I ever eat those stinkin' oysters? Oh God, what a night! I ain't never seen one like this before. He needs every hand he's got up there on deck and here we are, lyin' on our asses down here. Oh, when I get back to Baltimore I'm gonna kill that goddam bitch who said she had oysters. What a thing to do to a man. Just like throwing a belaying pin at the back of your head. Oh Jesus, it's startin' again."

He rolled over on his side. "Hey, skipper," he said weakly. "Get me that basin over there, will you? I'm gonna puke again." He felt the dizziness again, the ringing in his ears, and saw the skipper grab the basin and come rushing toward him.

Long after the flow of rotten, undigested food ceased he hung over the edge of the bunk, his body wracked with convulsions, gasping, gagging, tears streaming from his eyes. Through the torment he heard the skipper saying, "Atta boy, Bull! Get rid of it, boy. Get rid of it all. Get it all up. Get that mess out of your stomach. You'll feel better. Don't hold anything back. Let it all come up."

"Jesus Christ," he thought as he tasted the sickly, foul stuff that came through his mouth. "What do you want, my guts?"

Finally he flung himself back over on the bunk and lay still, his eyes open, breathing deeply through his open mouth, staring wildly at the ceiling. It was all he could do to catch his breath. He gasped and panted. He looked over at the pan. There was very little in it. All that work for so little, and such a miserable taste, such a vile, stinking taste. He nodded weakly to the skipper. "No more."

He rolled his head back and stared at the ceiling. The lantern swung back and forth on its hook, casting rapidly changing shadows around the cabin. It was more than he could stand. He closed his eyes tightly. He was conscious of the movement in the cabin as the skipper got Harry Bailey out of his weather clothes and into the lower bunk. "What a man," he thought. "I got to get up outa this bunk."

He rolled over on his belly, swung his feet over the side and dropped to the deck. Try as he would though, his knees would not hold themselves stiff, and he collapsed on the deck again. His head was spinning and he could do nothing at all about getting up. He rolled over and looked up at the skipper. "I can't do it," he said. "I'm sorry, skipper. I tried, but I just can't do it."

"Of course you can't do it. What in the hell made you think you could! Now come on, I'll help you get back up in that bunk. Goddam it. I don't know whether I can lift you up there again or not."

Between the two of them they managed to get him up into the bunk again. It was an odd maneuver, Bull pulling as best he could, and the skipper lifting first and then pushing. It was a clumsy thing and once they were both almost on the deck as the schooner lurched at a critical moment.

"Now you stay in that bunk. You aren't a damn bit of good to me the way you are right now. But if you'll stay there for a while you might be. And I don't need you right now, but I'm gonna need you a helluva lot later on. Now you stay there, do you hear me!"

"Yes, sir," he said meekly. He was in no condition to argue any more. He knew he couldn't get out of the forecastle, no matter how hard he tried. But he knew he was badly needed. And so was Harry. He remembered that Toby had eaten oysters too. He wondered if they would be alive in the morning. He had never thought of dying before, but he thought about it now.

Uncle John had done all he could do. He had treated them with the only medicine he had on board that seemed as though it might be effective, he had done his best to make them comfortable, and he hoped he had thus done something to speed their recovery. He had been living in dread since Harry Bailey had come tumbling down the ladder. He knew there was only one man left up there on deck, and that man was Toby Wheeler, who had also eaten the spoiled oysters for dinner. He had forced himself to put this into the back of his mind as he worked on the men, but any moment he was expecting the boat to broach to.

But now he was finished. He had done all he could, and all that was left was to wait, fight the weather, and hope that time would work in his favor, that the men would recover some of their strength. He turned and climbed the ladder as quickly as he could, eager to see the state of things on deck. He came out into the roaring wind and began to move aft across the ice. He could see Toby at the wheel, could see him in the light from the lantern that still hung in the yawl davits. He glanced over his shoulder and saw that the light on the *Hattie* was still there, but seemed to be a bit further ahead than it had been before. He hurried aft. "We're losing her, Toby!"

"I know! Wind is working around! Sheets need easing again!"

"All right! Hold her! I'll take care of it!"

He went back forward across the ice to where the jib sheet was cleated to the deck. He eased it gently until he caught the luff. Then it took in a little and made fast.

He was just turning from the deck cleat where he had eased the mainsail when the boat yawed violently. She was going around into the trough of the waves. He turned, a shout dying in his throat. Toby was on his hands and knees, vomiting on the deck. The wheel was free. He started for it, slipped, fell to the deck, got up and threw himself toward the wheel. This time he made it. He grabbed the spokes and swung the plunging boat back on her course.

During the entire time it seemed he never took his eyes off the lantern on the stern of the *Hattie*. Even when he was on the deck he was still looking for it. He kept it in sight and as he eased the helm back amidships and let her settle back on her course he could still see it, a diffused glow out there in the snow. It was the only thing he could see that was a part of the *Hattie*. No detail of her hull, rigging, or even her yawl davits, was visible. Just the light.

Suddenly he looked around for Toby. He was not on the deck by the wheel. His eyes swept the deck and then he saw him, crumbled up in a ball over by the starboard railing. He had been swept across the deck as the boat yawed to port. The bow plunged into a wave and the stern rose out of the water. Toby slid forward along the rail, almost to the point where he was hidden by the after cabin trunk. The bow came up, the boat shuddered, and Toby slid aft, almost to the big main traveler. He reached out, grabbed a deck cleat and held on.

Uncle John held the wheel and watched Toby slide, powerless to help him. The bow plunged again and Toby slid forward again, not able to hold onto the slippery deck cleat. With the next wave he slid aft again. This time he was able to wrap both arms around the cleat and when the next wave passed them he was still there.

For several moments she seemed to ride smoothly, and during this time Toby left the cleat and crawled slowly toward the after companionway. Just before he got there the next wave arrived, the bow went down as the stern came up, and Toby was sliding forward again. But this time he only slid as far as the cabin bulkhead. He reached out his hand and grabbed for the ledge at the top of the ladder going down into the cabin. The bow came up, but he was able to hold on and stay where he was.

He put one leg over the ledge and down onto the ladder,

then the other. He sat there for a moment, holding on to the door jambs on both sides. Uncle John watched him and wondered whether or not he would be able to get safely down the ladder. "Toby!" he shouted. "Toby! Toby!"

Toby turned his head slowly and looked up at him. His eyes were glazed and his mouth hung open. It was difficult to believe that he knew what was happening. "Dover's Powder! Toby! Dover's Powder! In my cabin! On the chart table! Dover's Powder! In my cabin! On the chart table! Take two! Two! With water! Two with water! Dover's Powder!"

Toby nodded his head vaguely. He turned, slid his tail up over the ledge and slid down the ladder out of sight. Uncle John watched him vanish, watched his hands slide from around the door jambs, and then he saw nothing more of Toby. He could not see down into the cabin to the passageway floor from where he was standing. He had no way of knowing how he had fallen, or if he had fallen at all. Suddenly he saw a small amount of light through the companionway and knew that Toby had opened the door to his cabin. So far, so good. He returned his attention to the ship. There was nothing else he could do.

Snow was still sticking to everything. The entire boat had become a ghostly white web of spars and the rigging. She plunged and shuddered, pitched and yawed. She was a wild, scared, female thing, going in all directions, challenging his strength and skill to anticipate what she might do next.

He was alone. A solitary figure on the deck of a 90-foot schooner, alone and already weary from the efforts of the last hour, distressed by the sight of his crew in agony. Alone and unable to move from where he was. He was bound to the wheel just as surely as if he was actually wrapped in chains and padlocked to the wheelbox. He was alone, unable to do anything except follow the light on the *Hattie*. Regardless of what was happening, regardless of its effect on the *Albatross*, he could not leave the wheel.

He looked around at the harsh unfriendliness of the now unfamiliar surroundings. The lantern hanging in the yawl davits was bright, and its light was reflected by the snow and ice, giving even more light to the distressing scene around him, forcing him to look at what was happening.

He saw nothing that reminded him of the soft beauty he had seen at home when the snow piled on the trees and bushes around the house, reflecting the gentle glow of the flickering gas light on the street corner. He saw a deck white with snow until a wave washed over the stern and swept the snow away, revealing glare ice, hard and slippery. There were no soft edges or gently rounded corners, only sharp edges of ice where the wind had blown the snow away. There was rigging coated with shiny, ragged ice, pock-marked and booming, rushing and heaving. When he looked around at the following sea he saw waves rise above the stern, saw the tops blow off into a fine mist, and felt the hard, frigid drops of water hit his face like icy needle points.

All that he saw was stark, harsh, and threatening, and his mind was free to dwell upon what was happening to him and to his *Albatross*. It was seldom necessary for him to think about what he was doing since all of his actions were instinctive, habit stemming from years of doing the same thing. It required no mental effort to stand there and hold the boat on her course. He was never aware of the commands his brain sent to his hands and arms. His conscious mind did not have to prompt his physical actions and was thus left free to ex-

133

plore the feelings of guilt that gnawed at him, to evoke any comforting thoughts it might have to offer, and send forth its basic strengths to assist him. But one strong, unswerving current of thought dominated all else. If he followed that light out there in the snow he would survive.

CHAPTER

8

"Eternal Father, strong to save,
Whose arm doth bind the restless wave."
From the hymn by William Whiting.

"I WAS ALONE, son. You're too young to know what that really feels like, but you can get the idea if you'll think about it. You know how it is when your grandmother puts you to bed in that third-story back bed room up there all by yourself? The house is quiet and you can't hear us grown-ups talking downstairs. All you can hear is the creaking of the rafters and that lamp on the window sill out there in the hall throws those shadows around the room. Don't it make you feel awful small and alone sometimes? You see things back in the corners and you hear noises and you don't know what they are?"

I nodded. He had me. I knew what it was like to feel alone all right. I could remember times when I would have gotten out of bed and come downstairs if I hadn't been too scared to get out of bed.

"Well, it was sort of like that, son. Only much, much

worse. 'Cause when you stop and think about it up there you know you're safe and nothing can hurt you and you're not really alone. But I was out there alone and I knew something could hurt me pretty bad and I knew what it was. It was all around me and I knew it was real. But I just had to keep right on going."

He needed to know what time it was and he couldn't see the clock. He had to know the time so he'd know where he was. He had to keep track of it. That was all he had now. There was snow all over the binnacle. Snow all over everything. He brushed off the binnacle, then he could see the clock. It was 2:34. Thirty-four minutes since—he had to stop and think for a minute. He couldn't remember where he had marked that "X" thirty-four minutes before. So much had happened in the meantime. Then he remembered. Just off Thomas Point. That was right. He had figured that in an hour, twenty-six minutes from right now, three o'clock, he would be off the mouth of Herring Bay. South end, probably.

He knew he'd never find it. Have to jibe anyway. No sense to even think about it. He knew he'd never make it. Not without another man on deck. He didn't even know for sure where he was. The only thing he could do was hope Tom Webster did. He couldn't lose him now. He had to stay with him.

In thirty-three minutes he'd be off Black Walnut Point. He wouldn't have to jibe to get into there. But he'd have to lay her broadside to the wind and he couldn't trim her sails. Might miss the mouth of the river and wind up ashore.

"Oysters! Oysters! Cursed oysters! I don't ever want to see another oyster as long as I live. Maybe I won't. Maybe I won't have the chance. Made my men sick, made me come out here tonight when any man in his right mind would be home in bed. Home in bed. God, it's cold. Home in bed.

Can't think of that now. It's warm there, and Laura's there, and it's cold here. I can't think about that. Only makes it worse."

He wondered why he had left her. She had asked him not to go. She had told him they didn't need the money that badly. And he knew this was true. He could have been with her now. He could have been warm in bed with her next to him. He would be warm and they would be asleep by now. He knew he had to stop thinking about that.

He tried to be honest about it. He knew he had wanted to come. He really had wanted to come. He knew it wasn't the money at all. That was only an excuse. His friends and some of his relatives were cold, but that was only part of the reason. Mainly, he wanted to go. Things had been all right until the men got sick. They would have made out. They would have been in Solomons before the sun came up. And the sun was coming up that morning, he was sure of that.

He hadn't noticed the cold before the men got sick. It was so easy to find all sorts of things that were wrong. It always was when things weren't going exactly the way you think they should.

He concentrated on the time. Five-thirty, six o'clock at the latest. That's when they would have gotten there. Three and a half more hours. If he had a crew. "If I only had a crew. What the hell, she might break up by then. I'm driving her too hard, but there's nothing I can do about it. I'm carrying too much sail. But I can't shorten sail. I'd need a crew to do that and I haven't got a crew. I shouldn't even be out here."

He hadn't thought he was carrying too much sail when he left Baltimore. He had her reefed down double and had come out without the foresail. It seemed to make sense then. He hadn't felt he was carrying too much sail that first hour after they turned down the Bay.

He knew he could do without the mainsail. He could sail her all night long with just the jib up there pulling her along. Of course he wouldn't be able to stay with the *Hattie*. He wouldn't be able to do that much longer anyway. He would lose them off the mouth of the Patuxent. He didn't have a crew to handle the mainsail and jib when the time came to jibe. Somebody had to lower the main peak. Somebody had to handle the sheet line. One man could do both. But somebody had to steer while that was going on. He didn't think any of them would be ready to lend a hand in three hours.

He knew that was when it would come. In about two and a half or three hours. They would be off the mouth of the Patuxent then and Tom Webster would jibe and go into the river and he would be left powerless to follow him. Tom Webster would run on into the Solomons and that would be it for him. And he would still be out there somewhere. He wouldn't even know where he was after a little while. He would have to run to lee all night long, all by himself.

"Damn Tom Webster and his cursed luck! He talks about it all the time and I can see why he does. He wouldn't have been out here tonight if I hadn't gotten him to thinking about it, and now he's here, sailing down the Bay like all hell's after him, and pretty soon he won't have any competition getting those oysters back to Baltimore. Even if we get out of this alive we'll be so far down the Bay we'll be lucky if we get back to Baltimore in time for Easter. He's bound to beat us back. So will everybody else."

He wished he could do something about getting some of the sail off her. He knew if it blew much harder he would lose the mainsail and it was a new sail. The mainmast was bent forward, even with the double reef. He wondered how

138

long it could stand the strain. The foremast was also strained forward by the pull of the jib. He hesitated to think of what might happen to him, dismasted in the gale. But he thought about it, nevertheless.

"Be a helluva mess if that sail was stronger than the stays and the mast. Jesus, what a thought! If that mast went down it would fall almost straight fore and aft. It would either hit the foremast or the back stays and carry away the rigging. Either way it would bring it down. Then what would I do?

"What would I do? Well, that's an interesting thought for a cold winter's night. It's amazing what a man's mind will give him to think about when he's cold and tired and alone. His trouble isn't bad enough but what his mind's got to start thinking and go to work to convince him it's going to get worse. Couldn't start thinking about how nice it will be to have this mess all over and done with.

"Well, what would I do? No point in fooling myself. It could happen. Christ, it's cold. Well, if it happened, I wouldn't have to stand here and hold this wheel anymore, that's one thing for certain. I wouldn't have to do that.

"I guess I'd get me an axe and chop it all away before it turned us over, if I could. What would happen? All right, damn it. Think about it. You haven't got anything else to think about. You can't think that in ten minutes it's gonna stop snowing and the wind's gonna lay down. So go ahead. Torture yourself. Think about it. What would you do? What would happen? All right then, think about it!"

It came with startling suddenness. It came with the sound of dynamite. Followed by a splintering crash. The wheel jerked out of his hand as she came around broadside to the wind. It happened in a flash and she was in the trough of the waves, rolling drunkenly, her mainmast over the windward side like the broken wing of a bird. It had acted like a rudder to turn her broadside.

He had been wrong about how it had fallen. It had not fallen forward, carrying out the foremast as well. The stays on the starboard side had held when the ones on the port side had parted and the mast had fallen over the starboard side, missing the foremast and its standing rigging. But she was broadside to the wind. Tons of water were pouring across her deck. He knew the first thing he had to do was close the main companionway. It had been open since he had come up on deck to go forward to take care of the Bull and Harry Bailey. Toby had not been able to close it when he went below. It had to be closed now. Snow was beating in there and had been. He was sure there must be a foot-high drift of snow on the deck below. He should have shut it before they broached. Now he had to shut it. He was glad he had shut the one forward.

Now he could leave the wheel to shut the companionway doors. He didn't have to worry about the wheel any more. He was glad he hadn't been trapped under any of the falling rigging. He had been worried about that. He was fighting now to keep from being washed overboard. At least she hadn't broached to on the uphill side of a swell and rolled right on over. "She wouldn't do that to me," he thought. "Now that's a romantic damn thought. But maybe that coal will hold her off her beam ends."

Water was coming across the deck by the ton. He wondered how tight she was. Pretty damn tight, he thought. Except for that companionway door and he had closed that now. But water could find its way in almost anyplace, and it certainly was having its chance to try.

He prodded around until he found the axe on the cabin

140

trunk and went to work on the rigging. Slowly he hacked it away. Finally the last shroud was cut and the mast went crashing over the side. Some of the rigging was still fouled on cleats and dead-eyes and one shroud was wrapped around the stump of the mast, but he cut them loose. Her mainmast was down to a stump now and all of that wreckage was cleared away. He fought his way back to the wheel. He had to get her back before the wind. Her jib was aback and fighting to turn her, and once she was free of the wreckage she came around.

"All right," he thought. "After I close the companionway door and get the axe and cut away the rigging and get all the wreckage over the side some way or other—it's an amazing thing how easily you can accomplish things with words when you're thinking about doing them. I don't even know if I could do all of that, and I was really cheating about the foremast. I don't think the main would go down without taking the foremast with it."

He wished the mainsail weren't so strong. It was new and a good sail. Best that money could buy. He thought it was funny how things work out. You go out and get a piece of equipment that your life may depend on and you buy the very best there is to buy, even if you feel you can't really afford it. You want to be able to stand up to anything. Your life may depend on it. And now his life maybe depended on it not standing up to anything, but being weak enough to blow out before the mast went. He had never thought of something like this. But that mast was one hell of a strong piece of timber. And it was in fine shape too, all the way down to the step. Not a rotten spot in it. At least it was last month when he checked it.

The rigging was good too. It would be hard to make a sail strong enough to tear that mast out of there. It might happen

141

though. But he was thinking he'd a lot rather lose the sail, even though it was expensive as hell, than be dismasted. But he didn't really want either one to happen.

He looked up into the snow. He was worried about the blocks in the upper rigging. He was afraid they might be frozen. "I'm glad it's snow that's falling and not rain. Maybe they won't freeze. Bull says—I'm glad I've got that man. I don't know what I'd do without him. Well, I'm without him now and I'm not doing so well, and I doubt if I can do without him very much longer. If I had him up here right now I'd be all right. If I had any one of them up here right now I'd be all right. But I think I'd even rather have Bull up here than Toby. He'd do some things instinctively that Toby would have to stop and think about.

"Bull wouldn't be awed by this storm. He's seen worse than this, I'd bet on that. On a bigger boat, to be sure, but he's seen 'em. Bless that little girl for not letting him ship out on a deep water ship. That's the only way I got him. If we get through this thing tonight I'm going to buy her the biggest, most expensive Christmas present in Baltimore."

He thought about the time again. He brushed off the binnacle so he could see the clock. Three-thirty. Two and a half more hours. Six o'clock. At six o'clock Tom Webster and his crew would be in the harbor at Solomons and he would be lost on the Bay.

If he had a crew he could get his crew to a doctor at Solomons Island. If he had a crew he could get them into a harbor and anchor until they got well. "What the hell, she might break up by then. God, she's pounding!"

"Old girl, I'm glad they built you." He spoke out into the wind, hardly aware he was speaking aloud. "I'm glad somebody took the time and the trouble to put you together well.

I'm glad the men who worked on you knew what they were doing and gave a damn about their work. It don't seem like there are many like that around anymore. I hope you'll hold together. I know you'll do your part to get me through this night. I hope I can do my part to get you through it. I'll bet it'll take more than this to pull you apart, won't it, old girl? You aren't going to come apart on me, are you? It isn't even bothering you, is it? You wonder what the hell I'm trying to do to you though, don't you? Well, old girl, I don't know how I got us into this mess tonight."

It was greed, that's what it was, he thought. And then he decided that he didn't think it was greedy of him to come out. He was giving himself hell again just because things weren't going right. He was feeling sorry for himself for what had happened. It was a hard life. This was part of it. They'd make it. They'd make it, all the way to Newport News if they had to. And they had to make it.

But it was greed. Any way you cut it it was greed. He had figured on making a killing on both ends. What was so sacred about that savings account? So sacred he couldn't have gone into it for Christmas. It would be a hell of a Christmas for them if he couldn't get into someplace before he fell apart.

He wondered how long he could stand it. He knew it would make a difference if he could move around a little. Go below and get a cup of coffee. Just walk around and move his muscles. He knew it really hadn't begun yet. He was cold but he hadn't started to get cold yet. It would get bad, really bad. He knew he wasn't cold at all compared to what was coming. In about an hour he would really be cold.

She was beginning to gripe a little. He could feel the rudder pulling on the wheel and the wheel pulling on his hands. He wondered what the wind was going to do. He wished he could get the mainsheet eased a little. He knew the wind was backing around some more and knew she should be running freer than she was. But there was nothing he could do. He just had to let her gripe. She wanted to go up and he had to fight her to keep her on course.

The snow was getting deeper. He thought about the snow piled up around his house. He wondered if Laura was asleep. He knew the children would be asleep. They were too young to know what was happening. But he didn't imagine Laura was asleep. And he knew she would be worried. What a life for her! But she had never complained. She knew what she was getting into when she married him. "Why she did it I'll never know, but she did it and God bless her for it."

He needed to know the time. The binnacle was covered with snow again. He brushed it off. Quarter to four. He caught a glimpse of the compass. "By God, look at that compass. He's heading right for the barn all right. He's got us aimed in the right direction, that's certain."

The course was right until they got to Cove Point. Then he'd have to ease her up a little and take a heading a little more to the southward. But at least he'd know where he was then. Who was he fooling? He'd think he knew where he was then. Think he knew where *he* thinks he is. That was a little more like it. But he would have to come south more than this. If he didn't he would go right ashore at Cedar Point.

He wondered if Tom Webster thought he was as big a fool as he thought he was right now. Probably not. He was probably having a fine time over there freezing his ass off and tearing down the Bay. Probably had never moved so fast in his life. "Lucky bastard. Everything he touches turns to money or luck or something just as good. I've never known anybody like him."

144

He wished he hadn't talked so much in the tavern. He wished he hadn't tipped his hand. If he hadn't, he could have backed out at the last minute and nobody would have been the wiser. But it was a good idea. He hadn't known about those rotten oysters then. But there was nothing he could do about it now. It was too late. It was too late the minute they came out from under North Point. He couldn't beat back against this thing, not the way this wind was blowing. Crew or no crew.

He was glad Tom Webster was out there. If he wasn't out there he'd be blind right now. Wouldn't know a thing. Didn't really know much now. Just knew he was following him. And that wasn't a bad thing to know. Tom Webster had been around a long time. You'd never go wrong following Tom Webster.

The *Albatross* had never moved this fast in all her life. She had never had anything like this pushing her. He knew it would be a hell of a crash if something stopped her in a hurry.

"My God! That was a wave! Almost lost her that time. She was starting to slide around for certain. Thank God they aren't all like that one. Got him too. Now he's got her back. I think I'm closing up on him a little. He looks a little closer than he was a while ago. Not much, not enough to worry about yet, but I think I am. I certainly don't want to pass him."

He had to do something about that main sheet though. It was getting very hard to hold her and he knew she would ease a little if he could give her a little more main sheet. He wondered if he could reach the line without letting go of the wheel. He tried holding the lower spoke and reaching. He needed another foot. He thought about lashing the wheel. If

145

he could lash the wheel for just a minute. That was all it would take.

He took a loop around the spoke and pulled it tight around a cleat. A little tighter. She would hold for a second or two. He turned and freed the main sheet. He eased her. She was sailing better now. He took a hitch with the sheet line around the deck cleat at his foot. He took the lash off the wheel. Now he could reach the main sheet and ease her when she needed it. There was only a little pull on the helm now. But he knew she wouldn't steer herself with the helm lashed. If a wave like that one a few minutes ago hit her she'd go right around if he wasn't there to fight her about it.

"Sure is snowing all right. Flakes are getting bigger though. Maybe that means it's gonna stop in a little while. That's what they always say but I don't know. Sometimes it does and sometimes it doesn't. Certainly be a help if it did though. But it wouldn't make those men get well any faster. But if I could see something besides that lantern out there. If I could only see a light somewhere so I'd know for certain where I was. I don't think I would feel so cold if I could see around a little bit.

"If I have to sail all night long it would help to be able to see Cedar Point Light, Point No Point, and good old Point Lookout. Lookout is right! That one is named if ever one was. Liable to see anything happen there. It'll be daylight by the time I get there. My father's there. I wonder if he ever knew nights like this when he was there. He must have been out in the open too. Cold and hungry. Poor man. I wish I'd known him, even for a little while."

He brushed off the binnacle. The snow covered it so quickly now. Ten minutes after four. He had been there over an hour and a half. Not a soul on deck but him. No one to talk to. No one to relieve him. He remembered four hour tricks that went by on wings. He had only been there an hour and a half and it seemed like a week. His legs ached and his back, in the middle, over his kidneys, was an agony to him. And he knew there were hours more to come. It hadn't really started yet. He had to stay there. He couldn't give up. They were counting on him. Bull, Harry, and Toby. If he couldn't keep the boat on the right course they would all die. He would too.

Laura was counting on him too. But she wouldn't die if he failed. It wasn't the same as it was with the men. But she was counting on him. The children, they wouldn't die either, but they were counting on him and didn't even know it. Christmas was coming. What a poor Christmas they would have if . . .

"It seems like all my life somebody's been counting on me for something. Crew, they always count on the skipper. Once they come aboard and leave the slip it's total dependence. I could be a rotten skipper and they'd have to do what I said. People I've never even seen have been counting on me too.

"Farmers sending their year's work to the market. They've counted on me to carry it safely for them. I've carried their corn, their cantaloupes, their oysters, their hogs. I'll never carry any damn hogs again though. That was a mess.

"And I've brought them things. They've depended on me to get their coal to them, their coal oil, a helluva lot of other things too. And I've always done it. That's what I'm doing tonight. Trying to get some coal to those people down around Solomons. I bet some of them are pretty nearly out."

He could have stayed in port. He could have dipped into that savings account. But he had never touched it. But he could have. He would have, but those people needed that coal.

He remembered the day that savings account started. Laura's father had given them a twenty dollar gold piece on their wedding day. Told them it was for the children's college education.

"She was a lovely bride. So beautiful. Everybody said so. Everybody always says that about a bride, but I thought she was and that's all that mattered. It was like I hadn't ever seen her before. When I looked down the aisle and saw her, coming toward me with her father, she was beautiful.

"I hope Toby finds somebody like her someday. He's a good boy and he should have himself a good wife. And it isn't often a sailor does as well as I did.

"We took the steamer to Baltimore and the train to Atlantic City. Left the old *Albatross* tied up in Baltimore, tied up at the top of the season. Man's got to be out of his mind to get married at that time of the year. But it was nice."

He wondered what Tom Webster was doing. He seemed to be changing course. But it was only a little and it was away from the shore and that was all right. It took a little of the gripe off the rudder. Made it easier for him to steer. He wondered what would happen if he tied the wheel down and ran down below for a fast cup of coffee. He wouldn't drink it down there but would bring it back up on deck. He could do it in less than a minute.

"I must be out of my mind thinking about something like that. If I moved fast maybe I could do it. I think I'll tie her down and see how she sails for a couple of minutes. Got to shake the snow off this rope. It's frozen again. Sure stiff. So am I. Stiff. My back aches like hell, too. Feels like I've been lifting something heavy all day long. And it never gets sore when I lift. Not ever. But it sure is sore right now. Right down in the small of it."

He got the rope lashed around the spoke and took his hands off the wheel to see how she would do. But she wouldn't do it. Every time a wave hit her from behind she started off to windward. He could tell it wouldn't work. He had known it anyway, but he had to try. The rope was very hard to handle when he tried to coil it. Stiff and cold.

He could remember the first time he saw her. She was sitting on the wharf at Point Patience, waiting for the steamer. All dressed up to go to Baltimore with her mother and father. He had just finished loading a crop of tobacco. Stole it right out from under the steamer. The steamer was coming down the river past Hawk's Nest buoy when they finished. He made up his mind he had to find some way to meet her. He didn't know who she was and she hadn't paid any attention to him and he certainly didn't blame her for that. He wasn't much to look at that day. Not for a pretty girl like she was. He was dirty and sweaty from trying to get the cargo aboard before the steamer got there. Bad enough to steal her cargo without holding her off the wharf while they loaded it.

"Old Doc Parrish was standing there watching us load. It was his cotton. It wasn't cotton, it was tobacco. Never loaded any cotton there. We loaded it a couple of times down in the James.

"But it was his tobacco. That's what it was. Tobacco. I asked him who she was. He kinda smiled and said she was his niece and did I want to meet her. I knocked ten dollars off his freight charges right on the spot. He took me over and introduced me. I remember how polite she was, so pleased to meet me and all that. Said she was surprised I was the captain of such a big boat. Said she didn't think the captain would be working with the hands to load the boat.

149

"But she got a real devilish little gleam in her eye when I told her why we were in such a hurry. She laughed at that and said I must be a pretty good talker if I could get a cargo away from the steamboat seeing as how Doctor Parrish had a nephew on her.

"I can still remember the way he laughed and said he knew her brother was mate on the steamboat but business was business and I was a pretty good talker all right but money was the best talker and I was hauling his cotton cheaper than he could send it on the steamer. And she said maybe that's because he's willing to get out and work instead of standing in the pilot house watching. And there was a kind of a glow in her eyes when she said it that caught me up short.

"We got away from there just as the steamboat was blowing for the landing and we got a pretty nice slant of wind coming out of the mouth of the river and were almost up to Chesapeake Beach when she came up abeam of us, on the starboard side she was, and she was standing at the rail on the bow on the top deck as they went by, and she waved at me. She waved at me. Big floppy hat on her head, tied around under her chin, and she waved. And waved. With a big floppy hat on her lovely head. My Laura. She waved.

"It was warm that day. Not like tonight. Cold tonight. It was warm that day, and the sun was shining, and there was a sparkle on the water, and the spray was white, and the sails were white, and there were a lot of little white puffy clouds in the sky. And she waved and she was wearing a big white floppy hat and we were hauling white cotton up the Bay to Baltimore.

"And everything's white now. Deck's white, and the rigging's white, and the sky's white, and the masts are white, and everything's white, and she's not waving at me tonight. She's rolling so much and I've got to fight her so much and hold on to this mast to keep from falling on the deck or into the water. I wouldn't want Uncle Fred to have to pull me out of the—what am I thinking about! I'm drifting off. I can't do that. What time is it? Got to sweep the snow off the binnacle again. Four-thirty. It won't be long now. And then I'll be alone. And I'm getting sleepy. And cold. That's why I was thinking I was up on that mast. How old was I when that happened? Couldn't have been more than thirteen. I don't know. Maybe fifteen. Seems so long ago.

"Cold that day. Still remember it. Nearly froze on that mast. Wanted to go to sleep. Don't know how I kept awake up there. Funny thing that was. I was shouting and counting and all that trying to keep awake. Maybe I could count the reef points on the mainsail. No point in that. Already know how many there are. Thirty-one. At least I'd know if I counted them right.

"I guess I could sing. Not much of a singer but it might help keep me awake. Nobody around to hear me so I reckon it would be all right. Maybe it would keep me awake. Wouldn't seem so lonesome, either. Be like whistling past the graveyard. What should I sing, though?"

Toby Wheeler drifted out of his restless sleep. He had been dreaming a fearful dream. It was a vague thing where familiar shapes constantly changed and stretched and compressed, and his mouth seemed to be pulled from one direction to another, all the time growing larger and smaller as his cheeks seemed to fill and empty. He seemed numb and there was pressure and pulling in his head. He was sweating and the corners of his mouth were wet with spit.

"Eternal Father, strong to save,

Whose arm doth bind the restless wave."

He opened his eyes and looked around to see where he was. It was a relief not to be dreaming anymore. His heart was beating rapidly and he was shivering from head to toe. He saw that he was lying on the deck in Captain John's cabin. The door was open. Someone was singing. Who could be singing at a time like this?

"Who bidd'st the mighty ocean deep,
Its own appointed limits keep."

He listened and recognized the voice. The door was open into the passageway and he remembered he had left the companionway doors open too. The wind was blowing the sound of the captain's voice down the hatch and into the cabin. He listened.

"Oh hear us when we cry to thee,
For those in peril on the sea."

"Jesus," he thought. "We must be in real trouble. I gotta get up there and help him."

He rolled over on his stomach, pulled his knees up under him, spread his palms on the deck and tried to push himself up. Nothing happened. He could not lift himself off the deck. He pushed his legs straight out, let his arms relax full length. His palms were down against the deck. He curled his fingers up into fists and breathed deeply for several minutes. There was no more singing.

He just couldn't do it. He couldn't get off the deck. He felt the dizziness coming back, the wave of nausea beginning to build again in his stomach. He opened his mouth and began to breathe rapidly and tried to control it. It didn't do any good at all. Nothing seemed to do any good. It was coming. Nothing could stop it.

When the fury was spent he managed to crawl away from

the mess on the deck. He relaxed and was still. The skipper was singing again.

"Whose arm doth bind the restless wave,
Who bidd'st the mighty ocean deep
Its own appointed limits keep."

His voice was clear and strong, a rich baritone. Tears came to Toby's eyes. His left cheek was against the deck. He wept. He did not cry. He wept. Finally he gasped for breath and then sobbed. The tears overflowed his eyes and rolled across his face and dropped on the deck. He was beyond control, overcome with anguish.

"Oh hear us when we cry to thee,
For those in peril on the sea."

CHAPTER

9

"Danger and death dance to the wild music
of the gale, and when it is night they dance
with a fiercer abandon, as if to allay the
fears that beset the sailormen who feel
their touch but see them not."
From *The Half Deck*, by
Capt. George H. Grant.

"I JUST CAN'T tell you how cold it was, son. I don't reckon
you've ever been that cold. Not for that long. But you
know how it is when you go sleigh riding and you walk a long
way to find a good hill and then you coast all afternoon and
it comes time to go home for dinner and you start back. You
think you'll never get there you're so cold. Your feet feel like
blocks of ice and you've got to go to the bathroom real bad.
You keep walking and the sun goes down and you can see the
house but it seems like you're not getting any closer. Try
singing next time that happens to you. I think it helps a
little."

He hoped none of the crew heard him singing that song.
He didn't think there was much chance of it though. Not in
the state they were in. Not with the wind blowing like a

fool—and it did wake him up a little, so that was something to be said for it, even if it didn't do anything else.

The snow flakes were getting larger. Maybe it really was going to stop pretty soon. It was beginning to look as if he might be right. "Hold her! Hold her! Easy does it, old girl. Almost lost her that time. Serves me right for thinking thoughts like that. No room for optimism in something like this. Just got to take it as it comes along. Can't start hoping for more than what's reasonable. That's the road to sure trouble."

The wind gusts were increasing. They hit with more force than before. He wondered what that meant. The seas seemed bigger and choppier, more confused. The tops were blowing off. The spray striking the back of his oilskins sounded like hail. She was becoming more difficult to hold on course. He wondered if he could lash the wheel and ease the main sheet again and then he remembered he had it made fast to the cleat by his foot. He reached down and eased her again. The rudder eased and took the pressure off the wheel. Just the effort of reaching down and breaking loose the ice on the sheetline had tired him. He knew it. He could judge the varying state of his weariness.

"But we're still afloat, by God! That's something to be thankful for considering the state of the men and that I'm alone. They wouldn't have much chance if I were to fall apart, but as long as I can stay awake and we can stay afloat, we'll just have to thank God for that small benefit. And every hour brings us closer to the dawn. Now that's a lovely sentence. Every hour brings us closer to the dawn. I don't reckon it'll be much of a dawn though. But at least it will be light and I can see."

He didn't like the way the mast was bending. Sail only

155

halfway up with a double reef and still it was bowed. She was being driven. He had never driven her like this before and hoped he never would again. He wondered how the men were making out. If he only had one of them to relieve him he could take a moment to stretch and get something warm in his stomach.

"Wonder if I can light a cigar in this damn gale of wind. Got one here someplace, if it's not soaking wet or crushed. Here it is. Feels all right. Now if the match will light. Clumsy work, cold fingers, damn near numb. Damn! Went out before I even got it to the cigar. Try again. A little longer. Please burn a little longer this time. Got it! Oh, but that tastes good. That's a damn fine cigar. Wish I could have a nice hot toddy to go along with it.

"Wish I was sitting at home in front of the fire with this cigar and a hot toddy. That would be nice."

He needed to know the time again. He brushed away the snow. It was an awful effort to get the binnacle clear. Ten until five. It wouldn't be long now. No more than an hour, but how would they know it for sure? If they were close enough to see it they would go aground for certain with the visibility what it was. The *Hattie* was less than twenty yards away and he doubted if he could even make out her light if she was much farther away. If it weren't for her lantern he wouldn't have been able to see her at all.

She was getting harder to steer again. Just wouldn't stay on the course. He talked to her and cajoled her and begged her to sail a straight course. And then he began to talk to Tom Webster and tell him to sail a straight course. He knew it wasn't the *Albatross* that was wandering all over the Bay. Tom Webster must be having his troubles too. That was why he was not sailing a straight course. "It isn't the old *Alba-*

tross, I know that. This old girl knows the course. She could do it on her own almost. As many times as she's made this run. But you've never made it in this kind of a blow, have you? Don't worry, old girl," he said aloud, "we'll find us a home somewhere. We'll find a place to land this coal some-where. As soon as the daylight comes we'll get into someplace and make a record turnaround and beat that old buzzard back to Baltimore. We can do it. We'll come sailing up that channel and be the first ones, the very first ones. We can do it. The *Albatross* and I will do it. She's a good boat, no doubt about that, good and true, like my lovely Laura.

"I wish she was here with me tonight. I'm not worried now. Everything is going to be all right. We are going to make it. I know we will. And I wish she was here to see it, this weather, this wonderful boat, see this life she's never really seen before.

"I wish the boys were here to see this. I should take them with me a little more than I have. Doesn't seem like I've taken them sailing at all, except when they go down to visit their grandparents. And God Almighty, they don't understand why we don't send them down on the damn steamboat. Ha! Where's the steamboat tonight? Ha! Tied up at the dock in Baltimore. That's where she is tonight. Not moving tonight, she isn't."

He decided he would take them all sailing one time next spring. When the weather warmed up and looked like it would stay good for a few days. Maybe he'd take them down to Point Lookout to see his father's monument. Let the boys sleep in the forecastle with the crew. They'd like that. He had never done that and he didn't know why. That would be fun and they'd enjoy that. "Wouldn't you, Jack?"

He looked around. The snow was gone and the sun was out.

The day was warm and clear. The boy stood beside him, looking up at him.

"What's that place over there? Why, that's Point Patience, son."

"No, I don't know why they call it Point Patience. Maybe some fisherman who didn't catch any fish there named it that."

"Those things there? They're whirlpools, Dickey-boy. The water is very deep around this point and the river is narrow here."

"One hundred and twenty feet in some places."

"How deep is that? Well, it's half again as high as that mast. That's how deep it is? That's about right."

"It doesn't seem so deep, Jack. Well, if you were up on top of that mast you'd think it was a long way down to the deck. Come back here, Dickey-boy. Where do you think you are going?"

"To the top of the mast! You can't go up there. It's cold up there and you might slip and fall. Do you see that wharf over there? Well, that's where I met your mother. She was sitting there waiting for the steamboat and I was taking on a big load of tobacco. And do you know something, she got on the steamboat and I followed the steamboat all night long in the old *Albatross*. Followed the light on the steamboat in the snow and it was so cold.

"Why is he turning again? He must be having trouble over there. I keep having to change course all the time to stay with him. He keeps wandering off from one side to the other. God, it's snowing so hard all of a sudden. I must have drifted off again. It didn't seem like it was snowing at all a couple of minutes ago. I must have been dreaming. I've got to stay awake. But he's having trouble with those waves hitting him in the stern."

They weren't giving him any trouble any more. He was handling her much better than he had been an hour before. He knew that. There was nothing to it once you got the hang of it. He was glad the crew was below where it was warm. He was enjoying himself up there all by himself. Things were beginning to work out. Soon the snow would stop, the air would clear, and then they'd see Cove Point light after all. And he could handle the main peak himself all right. Tie the helm down and lower the peak and then jibe and go on into Solomons. He wasn't even cold anymore.

"OUCH!" He had let go of the wheel and the spokes had cracked his knuckles. "I must have been asleep again. What was I thinking about? Oh God, I've got to stop this drifting off and thinking everything is going to be all right. Standing here dreaming about lowering the main peak and jibing all by myself. What a fool I am! It would take two good men, maybe three, with that wind blowing and all that ice. I've got to stay awake."

He had to stop fooling himself that things would work out as he had planned them. "It's the mouth of the Potomac for me, maybe even the Rappahannock. Christ, it could be Mobjack Bay. There's nothing else I can do."

His mother had always told him to plan things. He could remember her saying there wasn't any such thing as luck. That you had to plan very carefully and if you did everything would work out just fine. Well, he had planned this very carefully and look what had happened. No such thing as luck. His mother should have talked to Tom Webster. He'd have told her about luck

She had always said to have an alternative, just in case things didn't work out or something went wrong. Well, it had certainly gone wrong tonight. You could lay to that. "I wish she could see me now. I wish she could see all of this. If she was proud of me that day the block froze at the masthead of that oyster skiff she'd be prouder of me tonight. Here I am—I wish he'd stop that wandering—all alone on the deck of a 90-foot schooner, my own 90-foot schooner, carrying more sail than anybody's got a right to be carrying. It's a vicious battle with the weather. You fight it and you can't ever beat it. Eventually it stops fighting you, but you don't beat it. You never beat it. But at this point it's still a stalemate, and when you can't win, that's what you play for. A stalemate." He was talking aloud again.

He turned and spoke to her. She was standing beside him in the snow, but there was no snow on her coat and no snow on her shawl. The shawl was covering her head. She stared at him but did not speak.

"Isn't she a beautiful boat, Mother? Look how she drives along. See how she plunges her bow into the waves and raises her stern on the top of the wave? She's been doing this for hours and she could do it for hours longer if she had to. Listen to the wind singing as it blasts through her rigging, and feel the snow falling all around us on the deck.

"There's no need to be frightened, Mother. Things will calm in a little while. The men will be on the decks again soon and the snow will stop and the weather will clear and we'll see Cove Point light shining out across the water and we'll slip in around the lee of Drum Point and into the calm water beyond. She'll carry us safely to shore, Mother. She'll do it.

"I'm simply carrying out my plan, Mother. Why are you shaking your head? My plan was to come down the Bay tonight, following the light you put in the window for me to follow. The same light that has burned there every night. The light the steamers use to come into the creek. The lantern on the end of the wharf and the light in the window. Come down the river until the light in the window appears, then turn toward it, stay on that course until you see the lantern on the wharf. How many times have I done that, Mother? And I can do it this time, again tonight, in spite of this weather. Don't shake your head.

"We're going home, Mother, going home, following the light in the window. Or is that the lantern on the end of the wharf? It doesn't look like the light in the window, it looks more like a lantern, and it's not high enough to be in the window, it must be the lantern. I'm so cold and confused. I only know I have to follow it.

"No!" he shouted. "That's the lantern on the stern of the *Hattie*. And he's moving off course again. Why can't he hold a steady course? I've got to stay awake and follow him. I can't lose him. I've got to follow that lantern or I'll run up on the point and never make it to the wharf."

He looked at his mother helplessly. He was very cold. He needed something warm to drink, something to take the chill off. He was trying to act like a man and he wanted a man's drink. He needed a big mug of hot buttered rum, that was what he needed. He wished she'd take him in out of the cold and fix him a good hot mug and let him take a nap. He was very tired. But he needed something hot in his stomach before he could go to sleep. As soon as they made the wharf they would go up to the house and she would fix him a mug, and she must have one too, because he knew she was cold.

He asked her to hold the wheel for him for a little while. He asked her to let him sleep for a little while right there on

161

the deck. He would wake up shortly and they would land at the wharf and go home and then they could sit under the maple trees in the front yard and have a hot toddy. "You can do it, Mother. You can do anything. All you have to do is follow that lantern. We can't lose Tom Webster or we'll be lost out here and we'll never find our way. You can do it. Why won't you do it?"

He stared at her but she did not move. She stood in the snow and looked back at him but did not move. And then she was gone. He shook his head bitterly and then stared at the light. "The boat can take care of herself for a few minutes if I leave her to herself. She knows the way. I'll just get forty winks and then wake up. I won't sleep too long. Just forty winks will do it. And when I wake up the storm will be gone and the danger will be over and the air will be clear and the men will be well and we'll make the wharf and she will be waiting for me to come sit under the trees in the front yard and she will have something warm for me to drink. That's where she went. That's why she left. She went to fix something warm for me to drink! That's where she went! That's where she went!"

The light on the *Hattie* rose and fell in the seaway. His eyes followed it with a vacant, uncomprehending stare.

Suddenly he was jolted awake! Something was happening! He shook his head violently and tried to focus his brain. The last stray, lingering, wandering thoughts of a green lawn, the shaded blue-green grass under a maple tree, the white chairs on the lawn, the view of the river with a white sailboat lying motionless against the blue hills on the far shore, these last remaining thoughts were swept away by the pounding of the water, the rush and howl of the wind, and the crashing of the

162

bow as it plunged into a wave. But there was something else that had awakened him, for all of this had been there before.

It was a rapping noise, followed by an explosive roar. The main boom was rising and falling rapidly, the leech of the mainsail was rapping insistently, the *Albatross* was rocking back and forth from side to side like a skiff. The jib suddenly collapsed and then burst forth on the port side with a resounding roar, sending a wild spray of splintered ice into the air. He was going to jibe!

Instinctively he spun the wheel to hold the air in the big mainsail. The jib sagged again, collapsed, then burst out on the starboard side again.

The wind, in its movement around to the northwest, had now crossed over his stern and was coming across the starboard quarter. It had reached the point where it might suddenly flip the big sail and send it crashing across the deck, carrying away sail, mast, and all of the rigging. "Ease the main sheet!" he shouted, realizing that he would lose the *Hattie* if he changed course and if he did he would never find her again. There was no movement on the deck. He looked around wildly. "Ease the main sheet!" And then he remembered that he had no crew.

He was wide awake now. He watched the light on the *Hattie* recede into the snow. He had no choice. The *Hattie* had jibed, she must have jibed. He looked at his main boom, swinging far out over the water. There was still some room left to ease it, but there was nothing he could do. Perhaps the *Hattie* hadn't jibed. Perhaps her crew had eased her main sheet at the moment the wind had shifted and she was still running free on the port tack.

It made no difference. He looked down at the cleat and saw that it was covered with ice. He kicked at it with his foot. He

163

knew he would never free the sheet in time to do any good. Then he looked back at the receding light. It seemed that the air had suddenly cleared. The light on the *Hattie* was no longer indistinct and diffused. It was sharp and clear. Snow was still falling, big white flakes of it, and the wind was still blowing just as hard if not harder, but the visibility had improved, and it was now possible to make out the red of the *Hattie's* port running light as well as the light that was aft in her yawl davits. He knew that the sudden shift of wind heralded the end of the storm.

Then, for one brief instant, he saw two white lights, one higher and in front of the other, and one red light, low and in between. Then the high light was gone. And then, it appeared again, but this time it appeared alone, just as the other two lights suddenly vanished. And then, like the blasts of a double barreled shotgun, two loud reports came down wind, ending in a splintering crash. At that instant the bottom of the *Albatross* hit the sand, Uncle John was thrown against the wheel, and the white lantern that had been in the yawl davits came crashing down onto the icy deck and went out.

CHAPTER

10

"He has become a man in the full sense of
the word."

From *The Half Deck*, by
Capt. George H. Grant.

As UNCLE JOHN fought to hold his footing on the slippery
deck he could feel the bottom of the *Albatross* scrape across
the sand, push mightily for what seemed like hours, and then
slide off into the deep again. And for the first time in hours he
knew exactly where he was. He knew he had just passed over
Cove Point. Ahead lay the sheltering Cliffs of Calvert, and
five miles away was Solomons Island, his destination. Five
more miles and then safety, a doctor for his men, a snug
harbor, and blessed sleep.

It took no great imagination to reconstruct what had happened. It had been such a swift change, such a rapid passage
of events that he had not had time to reason them out as they
were happening. He had only been able to concentrate on
fighting against the wheel to keep from being thrown on the
deck; his only thought had been bare survival and the fervent
urging to his boat to push on, push herself into the clear

again, and he had not really thought of what was happening and its cause. But now he had the time to think for a moment and consider the sudden turn of events that had put him where he was.

He knew that the *Hattie* had gone hard and fast ashore on the point, rather close to the lighthouse, he judged, from the way he remembered the position of the lights. At the speed she was traveling he imagined she might have finally stopped with her hull pretty much out of the water, although he knew the surf would be pounding around her until the wind died away. She was probably a total loss, her rigging shattered, her hull stove in, but he doubted that her cargo was a total loss. He knew that the same thing that had saved him had also accomplished this beaching of the *Hattie*.

If she had been a deep keel boat she would not have reached the beach, which he was certain she had gained. If she had been a deep draft boat she would have been stopped some distance from the shore, the wind would have laid her over on her side, and she would have filled with water. She would have taken such a battering from the brutal winds and surf that her crew would have had no choice but to swim for it, and their chances would have been very slim. In a short time she would have broken up and her cargo would have been scattered, coming ashore as flotsam and jetsam, the property of anyone who found it.

But she was not a deep keel boat, and furthermore, her centerboard was not the dagger type that went straight up and down through her well and keel as a window raises and lowers in its stiles.

As it was, the centerboard was hung at its forward lower corner on a stud in the forward part of the well and came

166

down out of the well in the manner of an opening fan. Because of this, any pressure from an obstruction started near the forward part of the board and lifted it back up into the well until the obstruction has passed.

The board was very large and extremely heavily weighted, and did not rise easily, but Uncle John knew that as the *Hattie* came up the slope of the beach with the gale force winds driving her, the board must have retreated into the boat, letting her reach for higher, safer shoreline instead of becoming a fixed fulcrum that would first have thrown her forward of her bow, then off to one side to lie helpless and fill with water off shore.

The same thing had saved the *Albatross*. Her board had also raised as she slid across the sand bar off the point. But Uncle John also knew there had been another thing, even more important, that had contributed to his safe passage of the bar. He had been saved by his desperate change of course to avoid jibing. The sudden change had carried him out to the end of the bar and he had scraped across, leaving a few coats of copper paint in a furrow in the sand, but nothing more. He doubted if he had ever had less than four and a half feet of water under him, but heavily loaded and with her board partially down, the *Albatross* had needed a foot or two more to clear completely. But he had made it, the *Albatross* was still seaworthy, still plunging before the gale.

Nothing had really changed. Not as far as his own personal problems were concerned. It was still blowing a gale, still snowing, and though visibility had improved, even now he could not see the light at Cove Point, which he estimated could not be more than a half mile astern. With no crew he still could not head into the mouth of the Patuxent, and with the

167

wind shifting all the way around to the northwest, he was being forced more and more away from the cliffs that might have sheltered him, more and more out into the open water. He swept the snow from the binnacle and looked at the compass. He'd have to keep that binnacle clear from now on. He would have to keep track of his course from now on. Perhaps he could work his way around the southern end of Hooper's Island on the eastern shore, then get himself into the sheltered waters behind Bloodworth Island and sail south across Tangier Sound to Crisfield. He'd get less than he might have for his coal, but at least he could pick up a load of oysters in a hurry.

He stooped to the deck and picked up the wet, snow-covered cigar that had been knocked from his mouth as he fell against the wheel. It was still almost its original length and he knew it had long been out, but he had held it clenched in his teeth for hours. He knocked the snow off it on a spoke of the wheel and shoved it back into his mouth. As he did he detected a black shadow on the foredeck, framed against the whiteness of the snow. And the shadow was moving.

As he watched the man move aft he tried to identify him. He thought it was Bull Shorter, but he couldn't be sure. Then he saw another shadow detach itself from the forecastle hatch and start to move aft. Suddenly he saw Toby crawling up over the ledge of the after companionway and fighting his way to his feet. The effect of the Dover's Powder, and more than that, he was sure, the sound of the centerboard scraping along the bottom, had restored them to a somewhat shaky state of usefulness. When they arrived beside him at the wheel, Uncle John wished the lantern was still burning in the yawl davits so he could examine them more closely.

The wind was now northwest for sure and they had to jibe

168

now or run away from their destination. It was so close, and the choice was now his to be made, where only moments before there had been no choice, and the odds might now have shifted in his favor. He wished he could see their faces, but quickly dismissed that thought and made his decision to risk it. "Stand by to jibe," he shouted, and the men moved off sluggishly to execute the order. He watched them. They knew what to do, although they were somewhat slow in their movements.

Once safely around, the main boom now on the port side, the jib set and trimmed, he headed for the lee of the cliffs, where he knew he could count on relatively smooth water the rest of the way. Gradually the wind seemed to ease and the water became smoother. Without really thinking what he was doing, without having the idea firmly in his mind, he eased her up toward the wind, calling to the men to trim her close-hauled.

"Get the lead line, Toby! Go forward there and heave it! Give me soundings every minute!"

"What are you going to do, skipper?"

"I'm going back to Cove Point! Tom Webster ran aground back there and maybe we can help him!"

Toby got the lead line and went forward. In a very short time Uncle John heard him call out. "Deep four and soft!"

"Stand by to go about!"

"Half three and soft!"

"Mark twain and still soft, skipper!"

"Stand by!"

"Mark twain and soft!"

"Quarter less twain and hard!"

"Hard-a-lee! Smartly now!" He threw the helm down and the *Albatross* came up into the wind, her sails flapping, the water splashing confusedly around her. She fell off on the other tack and gathered way through the waves.

"Mark twain!"

"Half twain and soft!"

"What am I going to find when I get there?" he thought. "It'll be hell getting ashore. We'll have to launch the yawl—" he looked around—"and her cover's frozen solid and I reckon the tackle's frozen solid too, but I've got to go. I've got to help him."

"Half twain and soft!"

"On a night like this I reckon there's somebody awake in there, but you can't be sure they would even know what happened with all this wind blowing and the snow. Maybe nobody was looking and nobody heard those masts go."

There was a flash of light ahead, just off the port bow. Then there was another. He could hear the surf pounding on the far side of the point up ahead. Now he could see the light steady between the flashes.

"Mark twain and hard, skipper!"

He let her go on her course. He had to get in closer or he would be of no value.

"Quarter less twain!"

"Ten and a half feet. I can't go much closer. I've got to heave to right now."

And then he saw the lights. They were moving and they were down on the point, beyond the lighthouse. He quickly counted five.

"Ten feet! Ten feet!" There was a note of alarm in Toby's voice. The board was full down now and this was getting very close.

"Hard-a-lee!"

She came up into the wind. Ed Shorter was standing by

the wheel. Uncle John told him to hold her into the wind and he ran to the starboard railing. "Ahoy!" he shouted. "Ahoy there!"

He saw the lights stop moving. He could not see anyone but he sensed they had stopped what they were doing and were looking in his direction. He estimated they were less than fifty yards away. He heard the sound of shouting. He cupped his hands. "Can you send us a boat?"

"John! Is that you, John?" The voice was clear coming down the wind and he recognized it as Tom Webster's.

"Yes! Yes!" he shouted. "He made it! Oh thank God, he made it!"

"We are all right! Cargo is safe! Go to Solomons! Don't try to land! Go to Solomons! Tell Bob Cook cargo is all right! Tell him to come tomorrow! Go to Solomons! Load your oysters! We are all right! Do you hear me?"

"I hear you!" He turned to Toby. "Let's back the jib! Let's get out of here! Nothing we can do over there!"

The two men backed the jib and the *Albatross* dropped off away from the point. Soon they were under the lee of the cliffs again, in calmer water, making good speed toward Drum Point. But there was a feeling of profound anguish when he considered Captain Tom Webster's loss. It meant that there was one less sailboat under sail on the Bay. The death of a sailboat of 85 feet was a tragic loss, for the money she represented to her owner, the means of livelihood to her crew, but more than that, because she was irreplaceable. No one would finance the construction of a sailboat any more, except a yacht or oysterboat, with steam carrying a larger share of the available cargo every year.

There were tears in his eyes as he watched Drum Point Light appear out of the snow and then change from red to white just off his starboard bow, telling him it was safe to turn into the mouth of the river.

Robert Cook shifted uneasily, half awake, half asleep. He had been drifting back and forth between sleep and half-awake for forty-five minutes. Something had disturbed him, he didn't know what it was, but about forty-five minutes before he had suddenly opened his eyes and found himself sitting straight up in bed. He listened for a moment, then dropped back on his pillow. He had drifted off, then aroused himself, then drifted off again. Now he was closer to being fully awake than before and for a moment he opened his eyes and wondered why he should be waking up in the dark of the night.

There was something about the sound of the wind. He was aware that it had a different sound than it had had for most of the night. He rolled out of bed and stood for a moment in the center of the chilly room, stretching, arching his back, scratching a spot just above his hip on the left side.

He walked to the window, yawning as he went. As he approached the window he realized that the wind was now northwest. He stepped quickly to the glass and looked out. It was still snowing, but not nearly so hard, and he could make out the red glow of the light at Drum Point. As he watched he caught a glimpse of something else, and years of experience told him it was the starboard running light of a boat. He saw no forward light, no masthead lights, so he knew it was not a steamboat. It had to be a sailboat. A sailboat! Rounding the point and coming into the mouth of the river.

He hurried to the bedside table and struck a match, lit the lamp, rushed to the wardrobe and began to pull out his clothes. "Tom Webster," he muttered. "Either him or John

172

Talbott. Nobody else would have the guts. One or the other. Gotta get dressed and go down to the wharf. He'll have coal or coal oil, one or the other, but I hope it's coal."

He dressed quickly in the cold room, blew out the lamp, and hurried out into the hall and down the steps.

The *Albatross* lay alongside the oyster house and sank lower and lower into the water as the oysters were shoveled down into her hold. The wind was stiff out of the northwest, the ground was brilliant white with its new blanket of snow on top of the older, grayer snow, and there was not a cloud in the sky. The sun had melted the snow and ice from the decks and rigging of the *Albatross*, and Uncle John was glad the sun was shining for still another reason. The temperature was now eighteen. If the sun had not been shining so brilliantly the *Albatross* would have remained shrouded in snow and ice, but more than that it was downright comfortable, actually warm, in the sunshine as he huddled down behind the after cabin trunk with Toby Wheeler and watched the workmen loading the oysters into her hold. It was the first time he had been warm since he had left the tavern the night before.

The day had been filled with furious activity and the men had worked themselves into a gradually improving state of well-being, sweating the poison out of their rugged systems as they worked, in spite of the cold.

First they had unloaded the coal, doing most of the work themselves before the arrival of a group of hands to take over. Then, after the boat had been unloaded and the last of the coal just swept up and thrown overboard and the holds made suitable for the oysters, they towed the big schooner across the mouth of the harbor, about a hundred yards, to the oyster house, where they lay alongside to pick up their return cargo. Shortly after they left the steamer wharf they saw Robert Cook and a crew of eighteen men leave for the mouth of the river in the Cook pungy, bound for Cove Point with three stout skiffs in tow, to pick up the cargo of the *Hattie Travers*.

And now, as the *Albatross* reached close to her full load, they watched the sails of the pungy come from behind the point of land, sail behind the spindly legs of the screwpile lighthouse at Drum Point, tack across to the far shore, and come about to make for the harbor's entrance. She was coming very fast, close-hauled, heeling prettily as she came in under the lee of the island. She rounded up, dropped her sails, and with just a handkerchief of cloth on her, ran down wind to the Cook wharf.

After several minutes a skiff put off and moved across the harbor toward the *Albatross*. Uncle John could make out the big shape of Captain Tom Webster sitting on the stern seat, and recognized several other members of the *Hattie's* crew. He and Toby walked around to the starboard rail, and Toby caught the painter of the skiff as it was thrown up. Tom Webster looked up and smiled. "Hello, John. Wonder if you could give us passage back to Baltimore?"

He was rising as he said it, assuming the answer that he knew would come. He stepped on the middle seat, grasped the rail, stepped on the rubbing strake, and heaved himself up and over the railing.

"How are you, Cap'n Tom?"

"Oh, I'm pretty good, I guess. As good as you can expect for an old man who spent the night with his ass in the water. God, what a night!" He looked around at the men loading the oysters into the hold. "I'm glad you didn't have any trouble, John."

174

There was silence from the group of men from both crews who had clustered around. And then Toby began to laugh. "No trouble! No trouble! Wait'll you hear what happened to us."

He started the story and was interrupted by each member of the crew of the *Albatross* at least four or five times. An expression of growing admiration spread across the faces of the *Hattie's* crew as they listened. When the story was finished the men all stood quietly for a moment. Tom Webster turned away and stood at the rail looking out over the harbor quietly shaking his head. Uncle John walked over and put his hand on the old captain's shoulder. "What about your cargo, Cap'n Tom? Anything we can do to help get it in here? I saw the pungy was loaded, but there must be more of it up there, and we'll be glad to go around and load some more."

Tom Webster shook his head. "That's mighty nice of you, truly it is, John. But it ain't necessary. Bob Cook got up there pretty quick and they loaded right much of it on the pungy. There's still about another load up there, but I sold the whole thing to him as it stood, and you know something? These people around here are damn hard up. I got right near as much for it as if I had brought it to the dock. He gave me a damn good price, better than I would have asked. And he took it where it lay."

"What about the *Hattie?*"

"Oh, she's a wreck. Total loss. Nothing worth repairing. You'll see her when we go by. But her old hull held together enough to keep the cargo from going adrift. God bless her for that."

The sun was low in the sky when the *Albatross* came out from under the headland and met the force of the breeze as it

175

jumped off the shore and moved across the mile and a half of open water. She was close-hauled, driving, and carrying a bone in her teeth. She was bound for home. As she swept regally past Cove Point the men stood silently at the port rail and regarded the wreck of the *Hattie,* which lay in the shallow water just north of the point, close by the lighthouse. Spray broke over the wreck as the waves pounded it. Several of the men had tears in their eyes and made no attempt to hide them, others sighed deeply, looked searchingly at each other and shook their heads.

Both crews had vivid memories of the night before, but the crew of the *Hattie* remembered most clearly the way Captain Tom Webster was hauled out of the swirling, frigid water by the hair of his great white beard, muttered his thanks, then climbed right back aboard the wreck and stayed there soaking wet for the rest of the night in order to protect his salvage rights. In the morning they had watched him work along with the rest of them and Cook's men to salvage the cargo into the pungy's boats.

The time was 4:55, and as Seaman John Davis walked out of the radio shack he turned to watch the *Albatross* go by. He also looked for a long time at the wreckage strewn along the beach. At this time of the day he would normally have been fast asleep, but he had been too excited by the events of the early morning hours to even think of going to sleep. He was still elated over his first experience involving a rescue. He remembered it all clearly from the first moment.

At 5:52 that morning Seaman Davis had been shaking down the clinkers in the pot-bellied stove in the radio shack. He had just come in out of the snow with a full scuttle of coal, and it stood on the floor beside the stove. When he finished,

176

and the ashes and clinkers had settled to the bottom of the stove, he opened the draft to give the fire a chance to catch up, and then slowly stood, lifting the coal scuttle with one hand and opening the front door of the stove with the other.

The mere physical act of standing brought him face to face with the northeast window of the radio shack, and face to face with what he knew was the starboard running light of something where nothing had any right to be.

He stood transfixed and stared in disbelief for a split second, unable to move, unable to believe what he was seeing, and then the light vanished. Then came the muffled, splintering crash. The coal scuttle hit the floor. He reached for the pull-cord on the alarm bell, jerked it as hard as he could a half a dozen times, then opened the door and dashed out into the night.

He was proud that he had been the one to sound the alarm, and only he and Tom Webster knew how close the captain had come to drowning. Seaman Davis had grabbed him by the hair of his beard and pulled him out of the way of a large piece of the main boom that was being hurled directly at his head by the booming surf. It had been very close.

And he had thrilled at the courage of that redoubtable old man who climbed back up on the wreck to hold his salvage rights. This was the kind of thrilling thing he had only read about in books, and here it was happening before his very eyes.

No wonder he couldn't sleep. And then the pungy had come to take away the cargo, and he had watched as the men fought the skiffs through the breakers and moved the barrels of coal oil. It had been a thrilling day, but the thing that had impressed him the most had been looking up in the midst of all the turmoil and seeing the running lights of another boat in close to shore. The fact that someone would dare to maneuver such a large boat that close in shore in such weather was an act of courage he would never forget.

He watched the *Albatross* sail by the point, thinking how beautiful she was, knowing that the two boats had come down the Bay together the night before, and wondering how one had wrecked and the other had sailed safely by. Two words ran through his mind, a lesson learned from a text, and dramatically brought home before his very eyes. Two words that, in his young opinion, made the difference between the wreckage strewn on the beach and the schooner passing the point. He had read them many times, in fact he had read them again only the night before. "Eternal Vigilance."

The two captains stood at the rail near the stern, apart from the rest of the men. They had not spoken since they sighted the wreckage. There was nothing to say. The look on Tom Webster's face was one of utter desolation.

Suddenly he sighed deeply and said, "Well, she was insured, thank God for that, but no amount of money in this world will ever replace her."

"Well, that's something to be thankful for, God knows. But it isn't much compared to the luck I had." The word seemed to slip out before he knew it, but there seemed to be no other explanation for his survival.

Tom Webster shook his head. "I don't know, John. I just don't know. I reckon there's no such thing as luck when you get right down to it. It doesn't really exist, except maybe ashore in a poker game or a dice game. All my life I've believed in it, even counted on it to some extent, but I'll never thank it or curse it again. The day before we left Baltimore I signed on for the captain's berth on that new steamer that

178

Weems is building at Sparrows Point. They want me to take her long enough to whip a crew into shape, which is just about long enough for me, but I had to take one more shot at this Bay in a sailboat, figuring my luck would see me through somehow in a situation I knew damn well was risky. On the spur of the moment I decided to go along, counting on my luck. You decided to go after figuring out all the angles. I know you think you were lucky, but I'll just be damned if I'll say that luck had anything to do with the best job of single-handed sailing I've ever seen or heard about."

Uncle John shook his head. "It certainly wasn't very well planned and that's for certain."

"You've been planning it all your life, John. You know that in the back of your mind you had considered this thing happening and what you'd do. All of us have. No, I just figured I was too lucky to ever have anything like this happen to me."

They fell silent. Since the wreck, Uncle John had been a sobered, chastened man, a man struggling deep within himself to determine what had happened to his entire outlook. He was stronger and more secure than ever as to his ability, and perhaps it really hadn't been luck, but nevertheless, for the first time in his life he was acutely aware that there are some things over which a man has absolutely no control, no matter how carefully he plans.

A sick crew, being left alone on the deck to fight single-handed for stark survival, a shift of the wind that had threatened to carry him away from the light that had shepherded him through the horrible night, what cruel circumstances they had seemed at the time. But these were the things that had saved him. He remembered cursing Tom Webster and his luck. Had his crew been on deck to handle the sails, the

179

Albatross would have been wreckage on the beach only a few yards from the *Hattie,* her cargo lost beyond recovery.

This had not been the first time he had been forced to face disaster, but it was the first time he had ever faced it so completely alone. And he had faced it, fought it, and won. The knowledge of this gave him great strength, but nevertheless he knew that he would never again scoff at men who smoked their pipes, drank their hot buttered rum, and praised or cursed their luck.

CHAPTER

11

"The old order changeth, yielding place to new."

From *The Passing of Arthur,*
by Tennyson.

HE ROCKED back in the chair and blew a cloud of smoke into the still Sunday afternoon air. The steamer had left the wharf at Benedict and was on her way down the river. He looked at me and pointed with his cigar. "You know, son, it seems to me that a man only gets a certain amount of luck during his life on this earth. And it seems like you don't always get what seems to be your fair share every time. Sometimes you get a little, sometimes you get a lot. And sometimes, when you really need it, you don't get any at all. But everybody needs a little luck now and then, and maybe the Good Lord knows this and sees to it that we get some. But you never know when it's coming, so you can't count on it coming when you need it.

"Now you take Tom Webster. He believed in luck as much as any man I ever knew. To a certain extent he counted on it. But only to a certain extent, no matter what he might have said. And he didn't stand around waiting for it, and when it didn't come he wasn't one to curse his luck and stand around helpless. He was smart enough, and brave enough, and had enough experience so he just kept right on going in spite of everything, knowing his luck would catch up with him eventually and he could take care of himself until it did.

"But the person who stands around all day long doing nothing, because he thinks he's going to get a lucky break tomorrow, well, he's in for a bad time. Usually he's still standing around tomorrow. And the next day as well. He's counting on something that may never happen. And chances are he wouldn't recognize it if it did happen. And the longer he stands around the less chance he's got of ever seeing anything in the way of luck. The person who waltzes through life counting on luck never really has enough luck to amount to anything. And when he does get a little he's in no position to take advantage of it. He's just fooling himself.

"It seems to me that the man who really can take advantage of the normal amount of luck a man gets in the normal course of events is the man who works hard, plans carefully, and doesn't keep waiting for a lucky break. But when he gets one he can usually turn it into a big break because he's in a position to really take advantage of it.

"What I'm really saying, son, is that it seems to me you make your own luck lots of times, and even if you don't, being ready for it can make a lot of difference in how much luck you get."

He got up and walked out on the steps to watch the steamer vanish around the point.

As I said, I remember it best the way he told it that day. Maybe it was because I had finally seen the *Albatross* the summer before. I had walked her deck and held her big wheel. I had seen his cabin and seen the forecastle. And I had grown old enough, and sailed enough, to know what he was talking about. But maybe it was because it was the last time he ever told me that story.

He died that summer, early in June, on another warm afternoon. He was sitting on the porch talking to my grandmother. She was his sister-in-law, Aunt Laura's only sister. There was a lull in the conversation and then he said, very quietly, "One day that boy will see her under sail and then he'll understand."

The cigar slipped to the floor and he settled back in his chair. Grandmother said he didn't slump or fall, just settled back, and then he was gone.

He didn't really die though. Not for me. He really went back to sea. He had left instructions for his body to be cremated and the ashes to be scattered on his beloved Chesapeake Bay just south of the lighthouse at Cove Point.

He was right, too. I saw the *Albatross* again that very July, and that was the last time, and that time she was under sail. We were coming up the Bay from Point Lookout on a sparkling clear day, running with started sheets before a long-rolling southeaster, being pushed along with a good strong flood tide. We were almost up to Point No Point Light when we saw her coming. I don't know why, but I knew it was the *Albatross* the minute I saw her. She was close-hauled on the port tack and at first I thought she must be heading for the mouth of the Potomac.

She was loaded down and seeing her bows-on you could see the spray breaking over her and her lee rail well down in the water. She was really coming at us and she was so beautiful to see. Since she was approaching us almost bows-on, just a little

183

off our starboard bow, and it looked as if we'd both get to the same spot at about the same time, we came up a point or two so as to make it clear we would stay out of her way. She had the right of way, of course, but we let her know we knew it a pretty good way off. We were on almost parallel courses going in opposite directions when we passed. She was about fifty yards off to port, between us and the shore, probably about two miles off shore, and she was showing us a right good amount of red copper.

As she came abeam of us I climbed up in the main shrouds, my feet on the sheer pole just above the port running light, holding on with one hand and waving with all my might with the other. It was quiet on the *Natalie*, as it always is when you're running pretty much before the wind. It doesn't seem as if it's blowing hard and you can't hear the wind because you're moving with it, and you could hear the rush of the water around the *Albatross*, just as if you were aboard her, and you could hear the crashing and pounding of her bow as it smashed down into each wave clear as anything.

I counted two of her crew at the windward railing and they waved back and then I saw Captain Wheeler come to the quarter rail and wave. When he waved I yelled. There weren't any words, I didn't yell anything that made very much sense. I don't even know what I yelled. I think I just yelled.

This was my uncle John's *Albatross*. I knew her now, and I could believe all the stories I had ever heard about her. The quartermaster was braced holding the wheel, all of her stays on the windward side were taut, her sails were drawing everything they could and they fit like a suit of racing sails. She was the most beautiful thing I had ever seen, and the only thing I ever saw that rivaled her was when we went

184

to the Cup Races and I watched the *Ranger* run away from the *Endeavour II.*

I watched her go by, hanging there in the rigging, watched the figures on her deck get smaller and smaller. Suddenly the *Natalie's* bow went up and then smashed down into the *Albatross'* wake and I was soaking wet. My left foot slipped off the sheer pole, but I grabbed and held on with both hands as we smashed into the next wave. When she steadied and the wake was past I climbed down and walked aft, watching the *Albatross* get smaller and smaller. About a mile astern she tacked and went off across the Bay. I watched her go, thinking she would make a short tack and then go about again to go to the mouth of the Potomac. I thought perhaps she was going into Kinsale. But she didn't, and the last I saw of her she was still heading across the Bay, so she must have been going into Crisfield, or maybe further down the Bay on the western shore, maybe to the Rappahannock or the York.

I never saw her again after that. We were on the Bay the next summer and I looked for her, but there wasn't much moving that summer. There weren't many freighters going up and down the Bay, and those that passed us were high in the water. The steamboats were still running but the schedule was nothing compared to what it had been; there were fleets of tankers tied up all over the place, and there weren't but a few work boats around. The summer before, the summer Uncle John died, the last summer I saw the *Albatross,* was the summer of 1929, and after that things weren't ever the same any more.